SEAL'S VOW

IRON HORSE LEGACY BOOK #4

ELLE JAMES

TWISTED PAGE INC

2

SEAL'S VOW

IRON HORSE LEGACY #4

New York Times & *USA Today*
Bestselling Author

ELLE JAMES

Dedicated to my mother.
Elle James

AUTHOR'S NOTE

Enjoy other military books by Elle James

Visit ellejames.com for more titles and release dates
For hot cowboys, visit her alter ego Myla Jackson at
mylajackson.com
and join Elle James's Newsletter at Newsletter

CHAPTER 1

SEBASTIAN "BASTIAN" McKinnon shined a flashlight around the dark interior of the mountain cave, praying for something. Anything that would help them find their missing father.

"Why are we here?" Angus, his oldest brother, asked. "We've searched this cave at least five times. There's nothing left to see."

"They found William Reed in this cave. Dad disappeared at the same time. He had to have been here. He had to have witnessed them killing Reed."

"You think whoever has him, kidnapped him to keep him from telling who shot the convict?"

"I'm not saying anything. I just feel like we're missing something." Bastian walked around the cave again, shining the light into the farthest corners. "This is the last place he might have been before he disappeared."

1

"We don't know that for certain," Angus said. "He could have been swept away in the avalanche and buried under tons of dirt and rocks."

Bastian winced. "Do you really believe that?"

Angus shrugged. "No. Not after we found Dad's ring. If he was buried under rocks, that ring would be buried with him." He squared his shoulders. "I think he's still alive. And my gut tells me he's somewhere nearby."

"But where?" Bastian's voice echoed against the back walls of the cave.

He and his brothers had been home in Montana for the past two weeks, and they still hadn't found their father. A massive search had been conducted, but the mountains were so vast and filled with caves, ravines and valleys tucked away, they couldn't begin to find all the places a kidnapper could have hidden James McKinnon.

"The question is why would someone kidnap Dad?" Angus said. "If he was here when Reed was murdered, why didn't they kill him to keep him from identifying the murderers?"

"Reed stole a bunch of money," Bastian reminded his brother. "He had motivation to get out of jail."

Angus nodded. "Not only did Reed have incredible motivation, others would have helped him get out for a cut of the loot."

"If Reed was the only man who knew where the money was, and he was shot," Bastian turned to face his brother, "do you suppose he told Dad where he hid the money before he died?"

Angus frowned. "It's the only reason I can think of to keep Dad alive."

"And if he's still alive," Bastian's fists clenched, "he hasn't told them where they can find the money."

"I would think they'd be pretty impatient by now."

"Dad's a tough old bastard," Bastian reasoned. "He'd know that as soon as he told them where to find Reed's stash, they'd kill him."

"All the more reason to find him as soon as possible." Angus walked toward the mouth of the cave. "We're wasting our time here."

Not having found even one more shred of a clue, Bastian had to admit defeat. "Let's get out of here."

"We can ride up through the valley and look for tracks," Angus suggested.

"The rain and snow we've had will have obliterated any tracks from the day he disappeared."

"True, but whoever has him might still be hiding in the mountains," Angus said. "It's been two weeks. He'd have to replenish supplies."

"True. It wouldn't hurt to look again." Bastian slipped his small flashlight into his pocket and followed Angus out of the cave.

Angus reached his four-wheeler first, slung his leg over the seat and settled his helmet on his head.

Bastian lifted his helmet from the seat of his ATV. For a moment, he stared out at the rocky cliffs rising up around them and the forested valley below. How could such a beautiful place be so dangerous and hold so many dark secrets?

The distinctive crack of a shot fired echoed off the mountainside.

"Get down!" he yelled as he dropped to a prone position.

Angus threw himself off the ATV and lay flat on the ground.

Bastian low-crawled to the edge of the fat, knobby ATV tires of his four-wheeler and looked out at the scenery, searching for movement.

"You all right?" Angus called out.

"I'm fine," Bastian responded. "You?"

"Winged my arm but it's just a flesh wound," Angus replied.

Bastian frowned. "Are you able to ride?"

"No problem. The bullet tore my shirt more than my skin."

Bastian knew his brother. He'd claim a flesh wound, even if he had an arterial gusher and was in the process of bleeding out. That's how the McKinnon men rolled. "We need to get you back to the ranch."

"No way. I want to catch the bastard who took a pot shot at us."

The sound of an engine drew Bastian's attention to the trail that led west. The mountain jutted out at a point that allowed someone to have an unobstructed view of the mouth of the cave. And an excellent position to fire on them.

"He's making a run for it," Angus said. He leaped to his feet, jumped onto his four-wheeler and fired up the engine.

Bastian slammed his helmet onto his head, mounted his ATV and pressed the starter switch. He could see the blood on his brother's shirt. It didn't look like much. Thankfully, his brother hadn't been lying about the flesh wound. Especially considering he was going to chase down the fool who'd fired on them.

Angus took off, spitting up gravel and dust in his wake.

Bastian was close behind, gunning the throttle, sending the four-wheeler careening down the mountain path that was better suited to a horse or a goat than a vehicle. He held on tightly to the handlebar to keep the ATV from bouncing off the trail and down the two-hundred-foot drop to the valley floor below.

Ahead, a rider on a two-wheeled dirt bike drove the trail like he had a death wish. One bad move and he'd fly off the edge.

Though the rider had taken a shot at them, Bastian didn't wish that he'd fall off the trail to his death. They needed to catch this guy alive. He might know where their father was being held. At the very least, they needed to know why the rider had fired that shot.

With dust rising in front of him, all Bastian could do was follow Angus's lead and hope his brother was gaining on the man ahead of him. A skilled dirt bike rider would have the advantage of speed over the four-wheelers. If he didn't fly off the trail, he'd have a good chance of evading the brothers.

They hit a straight stretch on the trail and picked up speed.

Angus's brake lights shone brightly through the fog of dust as they neared an outcropping of rocks. Then he disappeared round the bend in the trail.

Bastian's gut knotted. He sped up, approaching the turn too fast to be safe. Then he slammed on his brakes and skidded around the corner.

Angus still held to the trail.

Bastian couldn't see what was in front of his brother but hurried to catch up. The path wound down into the valley below, twisting in and out of trees, following the creek that ran the length of the valley floor.

When the trail emerged into an open clearing, Angus slowed and stopped.

Bastian pulled up beside him, his gaze panning the field. He saw no sign of the shooter on his trail bike. "Where'd he go?"

Angus frowned. "I think we lost him in the woods. He must have ducked off the trail and hid in the brush."

Bastian spun his four-wheeler around.

Angus held up his hand, shaking his head.

Slowing to stop beside his brother, Bastian called out, "We can't let him get away with shooting at us."

"If we go back in there, he'll have the advantage. He'll see us coming and will easily pick us off. Or the other option is that he waited until we passed and high-tailed it in the opposite direction."

Bastian revved his engine, his frustration rising. "I'm willing to take the chance."

"We're lucky neither of us was fatally wounded the first time."

Bastian let off on the throttle, remembering his brother had taken a hit. He stared at the forest where the shooter could still be hiding. The only way he and Angus would be able to get to him was to sneak in on foot. By the time they got anywhere close, the guy could be mounting up and riding away, leaving them afoot, deep in the trees.

With a sigh, Bastian turned his ATV around. "Let's head back to the truck. We need to dress that wound, and the sheriff needs to know what just happened."

"We'll have to keep an eye out for someone who owns a dirt bike." Angus said.

"That should narrow it down," Bastian said, sarcasm dripping from his words. "If I recall, there are a lot of guys in Eagle Rock who own dirt bikes. Hell, we own a couple we used to race on the track out by the old quarry."

"Wouldn't hurt to ask around and find out who the best riders are. The guy we chased knew his bike and knew how to handle these trails."

"He also knew where William Reed died and was possibly following us out to the cave. Find the dirt bike rider, and we might find Reed's killer and the people responsible for taking our father."

JENNA MEYERS CHECKED HER WATCH. Her clients were fifteen minutes late to the scheduled viewing of the house and forty acres tucked into the trees at the foothills of the Crazy Mountains. She waited patiently, giving them the benefit of the doubt in case they'd gotten lost.

With little to no cellphone reception this far from town, she couldn't expect a call to let her know they would be late. All she could do was wait and hope they showed.

After thirty minutes had passed, she was done.

Jenna slid into her four-wheel-drive, slate-gray Jeep Wrangler and drove down the gravel drive to where it connected with the county-maintained gravel road. "Maintained" was a loose use of the word. The road apparently wasn't used by many, and it was in great need of repair. Many places along the road had ruts carved out by rain and water generated by melting snow.

Perhaps the Johnsons had come out earlier and

decided they didn't like the idea of driving down three miles of gravel road to get to the cute little house on forty acres.

With a sigh, Jenna turned away from town, instead of toward it. She had studied the plat map for this road prior to setting up the viewing. On the survey for the county road, there were several other properties even farther out of town.

Since she was out there, she might as well earn some pay in her part-time job as a private investigator. The insurance company that had covered Pinnacle Bank of Montana paid her to check out other properties for potential stash locations for the money that had been stolen years ago by the infamous armored car robber William Reed.

Yeah, she'd look for their money and earn a few bucks on the side in the process. She actually thought it was brilliant that they'd approached her to conduct an investigation. As a real estate agent, she knew more about county properties than most. It made sense to pay her to keep her eyes open for potential locations that might provide a good hiding place for the million dollars taken from the armored car in the heist of the century.

When William Reed had been shot, the bank's insurance company was certain all knowledge of the money's whereabouts had been lost. Still, they wanted Jenna to keep looking. Selling real estate gave her access to places most people didn't think to go.

And she studied county plats to understand who owned what properties in the area where William Reed had come to reclaim the treasure he'd stolen.

In the process of investigating to find the money, she could perform an even greater service in helping her best friend Molly McKinnon discover the whereabouts of her missing father. If someone was holding him hostage, they had to have him somewhere. A hunter's cabin, an abandoned mine, any place they could keep him hidden. And the Crazy Mountains were a great place to hide.

So, instead of heading back to town after a no-show, Jenna drove a little farther out to investigate a small cabin she'd noted on the plat map. The cabin was owned by Russell Mahon, a man who'd moved out of state ten years prior but hadn't sold the building or land. He paid the annual property tax, which wasn't much. As far as anyone in the county offices knew, the place was abandoned.

A perfect place to stash stolen money or a missing person...?

Maybe not the money, considering William Reed had ended up dying in a cave in the Crazy Mountains. He'd probably buried the money in one of the many caves close to where he'd bit the big one.

But to earn her investigative fee, Jenna would put in a little time looking over an abandoned property. It beat going home empty-handed after a day of researching places for the Johnsons. And if she found a clue as to the whereabouts of James McKinnon, even better.

She missed the turn onto the driveway for the Mahon cabin. She'd gone half a mile past it before she realized she had. After turning around, she drove slowly back in the direction she'd come until she found a turnoff onto a rutted path that might once have been a driveway.

Tree branches hung low over the road and bushes had crept in from each side, virtually obliterating the view up to the structure Jenna knew to be there, based on the survey plat. Unless, of course, the cabin had burned down in the ten years since the owner had been in residence.

Jenna eased onto the road and cringed as tree branches scraped across the top of her Jeep and the leaves from the bushes brushed against her windows.

A ripple of apprehension made her shiver. Her hand went to the bulge beneath her blazer where she kept her .40 caliber H&K pistol tucked away in a shoulder holster.

She never left home without it. Not since her ex-husband defied the restraining order against him and beat the crap out of her for leaving him and filing for divorce.

And being a real estate agent had its own dangers. As a lone female out in the wilds of Montana, she had to be prepared for anything.

Not only did Jenna carry a concealed weapon,

she'd also taken self-defense lessons in the Krav Maga art of self-defense taught in the Israeli military. Her instructor had been thorough, and she'd been a passionate student.

Never again would she be a victim because she couldn't protect herself.

Still, all her instinctive warning bells were going off as she drove down the overgrown driveway. When she emerged from the gloom into an opening where she could see the sky, she felt a slight sense of relief that was short-lived.

The cabin had not burned down, but someone needed to torch it. Paint peeled on the clapboard siding, and where there was still paint, the walls were covered in a thick layer of black mildew. The northside of the building had a healthy growth of moss turning it a yellowish green. In a sad state of disrepair, the roof was missing several shingles and was also layered in thick moss. Jenna doubted it held out the rain and suspected a heavy snow could trigger a collapse.

The cabin appeared dead and decaying. Even the windows were dark, as if the life and light had long since faded away from the inside.

An abandoned house no one could see from the road made a perfect place to stash stolen money or a hostage.

Jenna parked her Jeep in front of the cabin and sat for a moment, staring at the crumbling porch that dipped on one side where the support beams had rotted. She pulled her cellphone from her pocket and snapped a few photographs of the cabin as proof she'd investigated the site, in case the insurance company paying her investigator fee questioned whether she'd really been there.

Sitting in the Jeep wouldn't get her inside the cabin. She needed to see what was there. Granted, she wouldn't go inside if the doors were locked. That would be breaking and entering, and she wasn't going to violate a law to get a good look. That's what windows were for.

If she thought it was worth further investigation, she'd have the sheriff come out and take a look inside. He could go through the trouble of getting a warrant to search the property.

Jenna pushed open her door and slid out of the driver's seat onto ground spongy with moss. Thankfully, she wore sturdy boots. Too often, she had to hike around properties, showing potential clients what the land had to offer. Since Eagle Rock was tucked into the foothills of the Crazy Mountains, that means she had to deal with all types of terrain from open fields to craggy bluffs and boulder-strewn ravines.

With a great awareness of her surroundings, her ears perked to any sound, Jenna approached the cabin and climbed the steps to the rickety porch. As she placed her foot on the top step, the board gave against her weight and split.

She grabbed at the post beside her, which held her weight, preventing her from falling through the rotted board.

Her heart pounding against her ribs, she pulled herself upright and tested the boards of the porch before placing her faith and her full weight on them. The porch held.

As she approached the windows, she realized they weren't dark from dirt and grime, but shadowy because they'd been covered from the inside with black sheeting.

A trickle of fear slithered down the back of Jenna's neck.

Why would the owner cover the windows with dark sheeting? Or had he? A squatter wouldn't want anyone to see inside a house he was illegally occupying.

Jenna reached for the doorknob and gave it a gentle twist.

She let out a sigh when the handle didn't budge. Going in wasn't an option. The longer she was there, the creepier the cabin seemed.

Her instinct was to leave the property, climb into her Jeep and go home to a hot shower, a cup of hot cocoa and a romantic comedy DVD to chase away the heebie-jeebies this place was giving her.

She picked her way down the steps, avoiding the

broken one and reached the ground safely. Halfway to her Jeep, she stopped.

The front windows were covered, which made sense, since anyone driving up to the house would see them first. She couldn't leave without checking out the back windows. What kind of investigator was she if she didn't give the cabin a complete three-hundred-sixty-degree look?

Jenna pulled her gun out of her holster, flicked the safety off and held it out in front of her. She was alone...but not thoughtless. The cabin was just the kind of place those women who were too stupid to live walked into in one of those horror movies she refused to watch. She'd lived her own horror movie married to Corley Ferguson. What hadn't killed her had made her much stronger. She'd replace fear with action.

Well, most of the fear. Right now, a little fear was healthy. It made all of her senses hyper-aware. She listened to every sound, every creak of the cabin settling, branches rubbing against each other and squirrels racing from the ground to a tree and back to the ground.

As she rounded the moss-covered north end of the cabin, she studied the woods bordering what was left of the yard. No movement, nothing making sounds that shouldn't be there. Yet, she felt as if someone was watching her. For a long moment, she stared into the shadows beneath the trees.

Nothing moved. Nobody emerged.

Keeping a watch through her peripheral vision, Jenna eased around the corner of the building to the back of the cabin. The windows here were harder to see into. The back of the cabin didn't have the same porch as the front.

Jenna leaned up on her tiptoes. The windows in the back didn't have the same dark sheeting covering them, but all she could see was the ceiling from her angle. An old set of wooden stairs led up to the back door, beckoning her to at least try the back door.

Praying it was locked, she eased up the steps, careful to test the boards before putting her full weight on them. Reaching the top without falling through was the first hurdle.

When she tried the door handle, it didn't turn.

Jenna breathed a sigh and was about to let go of the handle when the door inched open.

Her breath caught and held in her lungs as she nudged the door wider, her gun held in front of her, her pulse hammering so hard against her eardrums, she couldn't hear herself think.

Nothing moved in the house, but the door swung wide now on creaking hinges.

She should have pulled the door closed and left in that very moment. Because she'd let go of the door-knob, she now had to enter the cabin to reach it. When she stepped inside, her gaze swept what had once been a living area. The floor had been made of solid planks of wood that had stood the test of time. The walls were a dark, wood paneling reminiscent of 1970's décor.

What drew her attention was the single wooden armchair set in the middle of the plank flooring. The chair itself wasn't what made her stare. It was the ropes tied to the chair that made her blood run cold through her veins.

In front of the chair was what appeared to be a car battery and a set of jumper cables.

Jenna stepped into the room, the gun shaking in her hand. She crossed to the chair and stared down at a dark stain on the chair's arms. When she stepped back, her boots stuck slightly to the floor in something sticky.

She glanced down. A patch of something dark covered the floor, and splatters of droplets of the sticky stuff spread out around the chair.

Blood.

Sweet Jesus. Someone had been tortured here. That could be the only explanation for what she saw.

Her heartbeat raced as she backed out of the cabin and ran down the steps. She had to get to the sheriff and let him know.

As she rounded the north corner of the house, she heard the sound of engines coming up the drive.

She slowed as she reached the corner of the cabin and peeked around the edge.

Two motorcycles drove up and parked beside her

Jeep. The men driving them wore black clothing and black helmets. They appeared to be studying her Jeep, then both of their heads turned toward the cabin.

Jenna ducked back behind the corner, her heart pounding. Those men could be the ones who'd tortured someone in the cabin. If they found her...

She couldn't get to her car, not with them standing there. With no time to plan, she ran to the back of the house and kept running deep into the woods.

A shout sounded behind her.

Jenna dared to look back.

The two men dressed in black had shed their helmets but wore black ski masks. They were running toward her.

Jenna ran faster, leaping over deadfall, zigzagging through the trees. She had training in self-defense, but her training would be useless against two hulking men. One-on-one, maybe. She wasn't prepared to fight off two men. And she might only get a chance to shoot one before the other caught up to her.

She wasn't going to wait around to find out what they would do to her if they caught her. She ran as fast as she could, going deeper into the shadowy woods.

When she couldn't run another step, and her lungs felt like they might burst, she slowed to a stop and ducked behind a tree, breathing so hard, she didn't hear the footsteps until too late.

A hand clamped over her mouth, and she was dragged to the ground and shoved beneath a bush.

She struggled to free herself, but the weight of the man holding her down trapped her beneath him and cut off the air to her lungs. She couldn't move and couldn't scream for help.

CHAPTER 2

JENNA LAY FACE DOWN, crushed beneath a man who smelled like an animal, musky and dirty. She could barely breathe, and movement was impossible. She squirmed but couldn't manage more than to barely rock the body lying on top of her.

All her self-defense training came back to her in that moment, but none of it would work unless she could free something…an arm…a leg…anything she could use to throw her attacker off guard.

The sounds of more footsteps pounding through the woods toward them made her go still and listen.

The man on top of her whispered a soft, "Shh." His breath was rank, nearly making her gag.

He'd tackled her and rolled her beneath a bush to the side of the animal trail she'd been following through the forest.

As the footsteps grew nearer, Jenna could see the

legs of the men running toward them. Men in black boots and pants ran past.

Jenna's heart skipped several beats when she realized they were carrying what appeared to be military-grade semi-automatic rifles. She held her breath, praying they would keep going.

Thankfully, they continued on until the sounds of their footsteps faded.

Once she could no longer hear them, the man on top of her rolled to the side and sat up.

Jenna dragged in deep breaths, bunched her legs beneath her and shot to her feet.

The man who'd knocked her down and rolled her beneath him pushed to his feet. He wore an old pair of overalls and a bulky jacket over them. His beard was long, gray and scraggly, and his hair was also long, gray and unkempt, like it hadn't been cut in a very long time.

He held a finger to his lips. Then he pointed in the direction the two men in black had run. He cupped a hand to his ear and tilted his head to the side, his eyes widening.

That's when Jenna heard a shout and the pounding of footsteps crushing leaves and sticks as the two men headed back in their direction.

She glanced around, desperate to find a place to hide.

The bearded man dropped down and scooted back beneath the bush they'd hidden beneath when the pair had run past minutes before. He waved frantically for her to follow him, a frown denting his brow.

Knowing she couldn't outrun the men in black, Jenna had to choose between this stranger and the two men.

She chose the stranger who'd hidden her the first time. Jenna dove beneath the bush.

Her rescuer, pushed leaves up in front of them to hide them from view.

Once again, the men in black came into view, still wearing the ski masks. Anyone who ran through the woods wearing ski masks that covered their faces couldn't be up to any good. They slowed to a swift walk, their heads turning right and left as if they were scanning the trees and underbrush, looking for something, or in this case, someone.

Her.

Jenna lay as flat against the ground as she could, afraid to breathe. The man closest to where they were hidden carried his rifle in his left hand.

Something about his left wrist caught Jenna's attention. A tattoo? She squinted, hoping to identify it. It looked like an elaborate snake, or maybe a dragon wrapped around his wrist. She couldn't be sure.

And then he was past her.

Though it only took about five seconds for the

men to pass, it seemed an eternity as Jenna hid in the woods with a bearded stranger.

Several minutes after the men in black disappeared down the trail, the bearded mountain man stirred, climbing out from beneath the brush. He held out a dirt-smeared hand to Jenna.

She placed her hand in his, and he brought her to her feet then let go.

Fully ready to defend herself against this one man, Jenna was relieved when the mountain man turned and started to walk away.

Relief rushed through her until she realized she would be left alone in the woods, with two men standing in the way of her reaching her Jeep.

The mountain man turned and beckoned her to follow.

She hesitated for a moment. No way could she go back to her Jeep. Not now. Not without backup from the sheriff and half a dozen highly trained law enforcement personnel.

Jenna couldn't remain alone in the woods, and she wouldn't be able to cut through to the road without risking getting lost or being found by the men in black. With nowhere else to turn and no one else she could trust, she set off after the bearded mountain man. If he was going to harm her, surely he would already have tried. Instead, he'd saved her from discovery by the two evil-looking men who could very well be the people who'd tortured some poor individual to the point he'd bled all over the cabin floor.

Jenna shivered. Who had they tortured? Had he survived? Why would someone do that? What kind of animal would do such a thing?

And was she insane to follow a perfect stranger into the woods?

Putting her faith in the kindness he'd already displayed by saving her, she followed the older man. "Hey," she whispered as she caught up to him. "Who are you?"

The man ducked his head, refusing to meet her gaze.

She gave him a tentative smile. "I'd like to know the name of the man who saved me so I can thank him properly."

Still, the old man refused to make eye contact, and he didn't respond.

Jenna grabbed his arm and brought him to a stop. "I need to know who you are. I can't follow a stranger into the woods."

The man met her gaze briefly and looked away, clearly uncomfortable with her in his personal space. He pulled free of her hold and walked away.

He didn't turn to motion for her to follow.

"I don't know where I am," she said, hurrying to catch up to him. "You wouldn't leave me out here alone, would you?"

He shook his head but refused to make a sound.

The mountain man continued through the woods without slowing to see if she kept up.

An hour later, when Jenna thought they would never stop walking, the mountain man came to a halt at what appeared to be a trail leading east.

He pointed to her and then to the trail and waved his hands in a motion indicating she should follow the trail.

Jenna frowned. "Aren't you going with me?"

He shook his head and motioned for her to go.

"But I don't know where I am," she protested.

The mountain man pointed at her chest, and then gave her the okay signal.

"I'm going to be okay?" she asked.

He nodded and waved her toward the path.

"But what about you?" she asked. "Won't you go with me?"

He shook his head and backed away.

Hesitant to leave the man, and unsure about where he was sending her, Jenna hesitated.

She glanced at the trail. It disappeared into the woods.

What if she got lost? What if the two men in black appeared and tried to hurt her?

"I'd rather go with you," she said and turned back to the mountain man.

He was gone.

CHAPTER 3

AFTER LOADING the four-wheelers onto the trailer, Bastian drove the truck into town in search of Sheriff Barron.

He pulled up to the side of the road in front of the sheriff's office, not wanting to get stuck in the parking lot with a trailer in tow.

Angus and Bastian climbed down from the truck and entered the office.

"Can I help you?" a deputy asked from behind the front counter.

Angus stepped forward. "We'd like to see Sheriff Barron."

"Angus, Sebastian, what brings you to my office?" Sheriff Barron stepped out of an office behind the front desk and approached them with his hand held out.

Angus shook his hand, then Bastian.

"We were out at the cave where William Reed's body was found," Angus started.

"And someone shot at us," Bastian finished.

The sheriff pulled a note pad out of his pocket. "Give me all the details."

Bastian told him what had happened, and Angus described the man on the dirt bike.

"Can you describe the bike?" the sheriff asked.

Angus shook his head. "At first, he was so far away I couldn't tell if it was a certain color. When I got closer, his bike was spitting up so much dust, it was all I could do to keep up without falling off a cliff."

"Any idea what kind of weapon he used?"

"He was at a pretty good distance. He had to have used a rifle with a scope to hit me," Angus said, his hand going to the wound on his arm.

"You need to have that seen by a doctor. Did the bullet lodge in the wound?" the sheriff asked, his brow furrowing as he studied Angus's arm.

"No, sir," Angus said. "It just scraped my arm."

"Go to the clinic and have them treat it. I'll have my deputies check around with some of the local dirt bike riders."

"Yeah, good luck with that," Bastian said. "If it's like when we were teens, there's a lot of those around. Not much else to do but hunt, and it's not hunting season."

"Unless you're hunting people," Angus muttered.

"Have you heard anything else regarding our father's missing persons case?" Bastian asked.

The sheriff shook his head. "Nothing. The trail has gone cold since you found your father's ring. We have the FBI checking into the lead your friend Hank Patterson gave us on the corporation that fed into Alex Tremont's bank account. Seems Tremont was the accountant for some pretty shady characters."

"And he paid the ultimate price for it," Angus said.

"Speaking of Alex, how's his widow doing?" the sheriff asked. "I hear she's engaged to your brother Colin."

Bastian nodded. "They announced their plan to marry soon."

"I remember the three of them were inseparable during high school. I'm glad Emily has someone to look after her. She's too nice a girl to have been caught up in all that trouble her husband was into."

"Colin will make sure she's safe," Angus said. "Could you let us know what you find out about the dirt bike shooter, if you're able to find anything?"

"You bet." The sheriff followed them out of the office onto the sidewalk out front. "We haven't given up on finding your father. I've had my deputies checking out hunting cabins, abandoned mines and some of the caves out in the hills." He shrugged. "We're looking, but there's so much territory to cover."

"We understand." Bastian turned toward his truck and frowned.

A woman walked toward the sheriff's office, limping slightly, her hair a mess, with leaves and twigs sticking out of the strands. He almost didn't recognize her with the smudges of dirt on her cheeks and chin. When he did, he hurried forward.

"Jenna?" he said.

"Bastian, oh, thank God." She practically fell into his arms, tears trickling down her cheeks. "I don't think I could have walked another step."

"What happened?" He started to lead her toward the sheriff's office. When she stumbled, he bent and scooped her up into his arms.

"Who've you got, Bastian?" Angus asked.

"It's Jenna Ferguson," the sheriff answered.

"Meyers," she corrected. To Bastian, she said, "You don't have to carry me. I can walk."

"I'll let you down, when we get inside." He nodded toward his brother. "Door."

Angus hurried toward the door and pulled it open.

Bastian carried Jenna inside.

"Take her into my office," the sheriff said. "You can set her on the couch in there."

Bastian stepped around the front desk and marched down the hallway to the last door on the right. Inside the sheriff's office, he eased Jenna onto the couch and sat beside her, slipped his arm around her shoulders and pulled her against him. "What happened?"

Jenna gave him a weak smile. "Nice to see you, too." She looked past him to Angus and the sheriff. "I'm just glad I made it back to town. Could I get a drink of water?"

"I'll get you some." Angus left the room and returned with a bottle of water.

Jenna drank half of it before she finally pushed away from Bastian and straightened her shoulders. "I was out on Black Water Road to show a property to a family who, by the way, didn't show. Since I was out there, I drove a little farther down the road to a cabin owned by Russell Mahon. I understand he's been gone from Montana for ten years. I thought I'd check it out for a possible listing, since he hasn't bothered with it for a decade."

"And you had to trailblaze through the woods to get to it?" Bastian asked, impatient for her to get to the reason why she was so messed up and exhausted.

She frowned. "I'm getting to that. Anyway, the place was overgrown and dark. Really dark. Someone had hung black sheeting in the front windows. Which I thought strange. The front door was locked, so I went to the back of the cabin and the windows weren't covered, nor was the back door closed properly." She drew in a deep breath, her face growing pale.

Bastian's gut clenched, but he didn't say anything, letting her get to the point on her own.

"There was a chair inside, with ropes, a car battery and jumper cables." Her gaze met the sheriff's. "And the floor was sticky. I think it was covered in blood."

Angus swore.

Bastian's heart stopped beating for a long moment, and then pounded hard against his ribs. He stood. "Where was the cabin? Black Water Road?" he started for the door.

"Wait," she grabbed his arm. "There's more."

Bastian returned to sit beside her, holding her hand.

"I heard engines coming up the drive, so I went back around the cabin to see who was coming. Two men drove up on motorcycles. They parked beside my Jeep. I couldn't get to my vehicle." Her eyes filled. "I was afraid if they were the ones who'd been inside the cabin… Well, I was afraid, so I ran."

"You did the right thing," Bastian said.

She nodded. "I know that now. I ran into the woods. They came after me. When I couldn't run anymore, I hid behind a tree. Then a man grabbed me from behind and threw me under a bush."

Bastian's free hand clenched into a fist. That would explain her disheveled appearance. "One of the men from the motorcycles?"

She shook her head. "No, he was a…a mountain

31

man with a long beard. He hid me from the two men. They ran right past us, and they were carrying guns. Rifles like they use in the military."

"Who was the man who hid you?" Bastian asked.

"I don't know. He didn't talk. He just pointed and urged me to follow him. I couldn't go back to my Jeep. Not when those men might be waiting for me to return. I didn't have a choice but to follow the bearded mountain man. He saved my life."

"How did you get here?" the sheriff asked.

"I followed him through the hills for what felt like forever, until we came to a trail that led into town. It led to the road out by the cemetery. I came straight here." She held the sheriff's gaze. "You had to know about the cabin. I think someone was tortured there."

Bastian met Angus's gaze. "Dad."

Angus turned to the sheriff. "We have to get out there."

Bastian rose to stand beside his brother. "The sooner the better."

"Let me call in a couple of my deputies. You can't go out there alone. Not if those men are heavily armed."

"How long ago was this?" Bastian asked Jenna.

She glanced at her watch. "About four hours ago."

Sheriff Barron stepped out of the office to put out a call for his deputies on patrol to head out to the Mahon place on Black Water Road.

Angus pulled out his cellphone. "Colin and Duncan need to know. They'll want to be there."

Bastian paced in front of the sheriff's desk, his stomach roiling at the thought of their father being subjected to torture. "We have to find him."

Angus nodded, pressing the phone to his ear. "Mom, give me Colin or Duncan. No time to explain. I just need one or the other."

Sebastian understood why he didn't want to tell their mother anything yet. She'd be beside herself if she knew her husband had been tortured.

"Duncan," Angus said. "Get Colin and meet us at the turnoff onto Black Water Road. I'll explain when you get there." He ended the call and glanced at Bastian. "Ready?"

Bastian nodded.

Jenna pushed to her feet. "I'm going with you."

"No," Bastian said. "It's too dangerous."

Jenna's eyes narrowed. "I know it's dangerous. I was there. But you don't know where the turnoff is. The driveway is overgrown." She squared her shoulders and lifted her chin. "And my Jeep is out there."

"Bring her," the sheriff said from the door. "My men and I will go in first and clear the site before we let you and your brothers in."

Bastian didn't like the idea of Jenna going with them, but he didn't argue with the sheriff.

The sheriff led the way out of the office. "My men are on their way out to Black Water Road. I told them to meet me at the highway turnoff. Like I said, we'll go in first." He climbed into his service SUV.

"I'll drive," Angus said and hopped into the driver's seat.

Bastian held the door open for Jenna to climb into the back seat behind Angus. Then he hurried around to the passenger seat.

He'd barely closed his door when Angus shifted into gear and followed the sheriff out to the highway.

Bastian turned in his seat, realizing for the first time, he hadn't bothered to ask if she was all right. "You're Molly's friend, aren't you?"

JENNA'S GAZE met Bastian's. "Yes, I'm Molly's friend." That he could forget so easily sent her straight back to her high school days when she'd been in love with him, and he had only known her as his kid sister's little friend, if he'd recognized her at all.

Bastian McKinnon had been Jenna's world. High school football player, motorcycle riding bad boy with a really big heart.

He'd looked and acted tough, but she'd watched him nurse a horse back to health, play with a kitten and hug his favorite dog. And he was good to his little sister, even when she tagged along with her friend.

Bastian McKinnon had been the man Jenna had set her bar on. But he was in love with his high school sweetheart, Lauren. They'd been inseparable throughout high school. They'd even talked about going to the same college when they graduated.

Only Lauren didn't make it to graduation. One night, one drunk driver and a head-on collision sent Bastian and Lauren to the hospital. Bastian was treated and released. Lauren died of massive internal injuries. She hadn't been wearing her seatbelt, and she'd been thrown through the windshield.

Jenna remembered Bastian's face at Lauren's funeral. Stone cold and haggard beyond his eighteen years. He'd blamed himself more than the drunk driver who'd hit them.

Instead of college, Bastian enlisted in the Navy and drove himself hard during basic. His drill sergeant noticed and recommended him for the Navy SEALs BUD/S training.

Bastian hadn't been back home often. He made it every other year to visit his parents, but he didn't stay long. And he laid flowers on Lauren's grave. After all those years, he hadn't forgotten.

Jenna sighed. After Bastian left Eagle Rock, Jenna had given up any pretense of ever getting him to fall in love with, much less notice, her. She went on to date Corley Ferguson, a football player who had a full-ride scholarship to play college football for Montana State.

"The sheriff called you Jenna Ferguson. I thought

your last name was Meyers," Angus said, glancing back at her through the rearview mirror.

"It is Meyers. I'm divorced," she said. "I reverted to my maiden name."

"Ferguson…" Bastian's eyes narrowed. "I played football with a Ferguson. Otis." His gaze met hers.

"Not the same one. I married Corley, Otis's younger brother."

"Sorry it didn't work out," Bastian said.

"Don't be. I'm not." Jenna looked away. She'd suffered enough during the seven years they'd been together.

"So, you're a realtor?" Angus asked.

"I am."

"How long have you been doing that?" Angus asked, but it was Bastian's gaze she met.

"A little more than a year." She'd studied hard while she was still married to Corley, hiding her books from him. He hadn't wanted her to work outside the home, insisting she needed to cook, clean and focus on bringing him a beer when he demanded one. A job outside the home would make her far too independent.

Corley had a hard time keeping a job.

Jenna had married him right out of high school and followed him to Bozeman and Montana State University. His temper lost him the scholarship during the first semester he was there. After that, his dreams of playing for the NFL were over. He'd returned to Eagle Rock and got the only job he could find, working at the feed store, slinging fifty-pound sacks of horse and chicken feed.

She should have cut her losses then, but Jenna had promised to love, honor and cherish her husband through richer and poorer.

Life wouldn't have been as hard, had Corley allowed her to get a job. He'd insisted he could support them both. But the money was tight. They'd ended up renting a rundown trailer on the edge of town. Between the cold during the winter and the mice infestation, Jenna had never been more miserable.

She'd stayed with him through the first few years, mostly because she didn't want to admit she'd made a mistake. During the last years of her marriage, she'd stayed because she didn't have a way to support herself.

Until she'd found the course on how to get her real estate license.

Not all the years were bad. It wasn't until Corley started drinking a case of beer every three days that Jenna's misery escalated.

Corley was a mean drunk. He'd come home from the bar, having spent his paycheck buying rounds he couldn't afford for the rest of his beer-drinking buddies.

When he came through the door, he'd pick a fight

with her and end up slapping her around, and then forcing her to have sex.

Sometimes, he stayed out all night.

Those were the nights Jenna loved and hated. She loved that she didn't have to put up with him but hated not knowing when he'd show up to hit her again.

One night she'd fallen asleep over her coursework. Corley came home earlier than usual and found her with her study materials. He'd exploded in a rage so violent, Jenna hadn't thought she'd live through it.

He'd thrown her book at her head, catching her right cheek. Corley yelled, punched her in the belly and the face several times. When she fell to the ground, he'd kicked her in the side over and over, breaking several of her ribs.

He'd left her half-conscious on the floor and gone back out to the bar.

Jenna lay for a long time, trying to bring air into her lungs. When she could muster the strength, she'd dragged herself to the phone, dialed 911, gave her address and promptly passed out.

She woke when the EMTs loaded her onto a gurney and wheeled her out.

Corley arrived in time to ask where the hell they were taking her.

She'd answered, "Away from you."

He'd lunged toward the EMT and would have

punched him, but a sheriff's deputy grabbed him and zip-tied his wrists behind his back.

Once at the hospital, Jenna had asked that they not allow her husband in to visit. Her parents had moved to Florida a couple of years earlier. She didn't want to upset them and make them spend the money it would take to fly out to Montana to be with her. When the nurse asked who she'd like to notify, the only person she could think of was her best friend from high school, Molly McKinnon.

Molly had come immediately, remaining by her side throughout her stay in the hospital. She'd insisted on Jenna coming home to the Iron Horse Ranch where Molly lived with her father and mother. For the next couple of weeks, the McKinnons had helped her get back on her feet, physically and emotionally.

Molly had been the one to introduce her to her Krav Maga trainer in Bozeman. Twice a week, she drove Jenna to take the classes with her.

Molly had helped Jenna study for her real estate exam. She passed on her first attempt and landed a job with a local firm.

On her first day at the job, Corley showed up in the office and demanded she get her ass home.

Jenna had stood up to him, with just a few Krav Maga lessons under her belt. Not at all confident in her abilities to take down a man twice her weight.

When she knocked him flat on his ass, he bellowed like an angry bull and came at her.

She'd dodged him, he hit a wall and lay still long enough for her to get outside and flag down a passing sheriff's deputy. Afterward, she got the county judge to put a restraining order on Corley. He wasn't to come within twenty yards of her, call her or talk to her.

She'd purchased a gun and was willing to use it if he ever tried to hurt her again.

"They're all here," Angus said, pulling Jenna out of the past and back to the present and the horrific setting she'd witnessed inside the Mahon cabin.

Colin and Duncan were waiting in Colin's pickup. When they saw Angus turn off onto Black Water Road, they got out. Colin rounded to the driver's side, Duncan to the passenger side as Angus and Bastian lowered their windows.

Bastian gave them a brief situation report ending with, "Someone was tortured in that cabin."

Colin and Duncan's jaws both tightened.

"You think it was Dad?" Duncan asked.

Bastian drew in a breath and let it out. "We don't know. Whoever it was needs help. If it's Dad, likely he's still alive."

Sheriff Barron left his vehicle and walked up to the driver's side of their pickup. Acknowledging Colin with a nod, he turned to Angus. "We'll let you lead the way. Once you arrive at the turnoff, stay on this road, just pull forward. Let us go in." He looked over Angus's shoulder, capturing Jenna's glance. "Got it?"

She nodded. "Got it."

Colin and Duncan hurried back to their truck while Angus pulled ahead of the convoy and drove slowly down Black Water Road.

Jenna slid across the back seat and stared out the window, trying to remember what the entry to the cabin's driveway had looked like.

"Do you need to sit up front?" Bastian asked.

"Actually, yes. But don't stop. I don't want you to slow down."

"We're going slow enough, you can crawl up through the middle with no problem," Angus said. "I promise not to slam on the brakes."

Bastian frowned. "It wouldn't take a minute to stop and let her go around."

Jenna was halfway across the console already, her gaze on the road ahead as she slipped her leg across Bastian's.

"Sorry," she said. "I don't think it's much further. I remember that dead tree on the right."

The truck's front right wheel hit a rut. Jenna slipped on the console and bumped her head against the ceiling.

"Damn it, woman." Bastian grabbed her hips and pulled her down.

She sat hard on Bastian's lap.

"You need to be wearing a seatbelt," he grumbled. He reached between them, unhooked the belt he wore and pulled it around to encircle both of them, his arm clamped around her middle to feed the metal into the buckle. Once it was clipped in place, he continued to hold her around her middle.

Distracted by the arm around her middle and the warmth of his body beneath her, Jenna almost missed the turn. The front bumper had passed it when she recognized the area. "There!" she cried out and pointed out the passenger window. "It's there."

Angus continued past the driveway and stopped when the trailer he was pulling cleared the entrance.

The sheriff parked his vehicle and got out, drawing his weapon from the holster at his side. He nodded to the deputies.

They disappeared on foot into the heavily overgrown driveway, leading up to the cabin.

Jenna didn't move. She was almost afraid to breathe, listening through Bastian's open window for sounds of gunfire, shouts or anything that would indicate what was happening at the cabin.

After what felt like forever, a deputy materialized out of the woods and walked over to their truck. "Sheriff Barron said you could come to the cabin."

Jenna flung open the door.

Bastian unbuckled the seatbelt and helped her down from the truck.

Once on the ground, Jenna touched her hand to

the gun beneath her jacket, comforted by its presence. When Bastian slipped an arm around her waist, she felt even better, knowing someone had her back. She liked the feel of his hand on her side. It wasn't obsessively possessive, just reassuring and warm.

As she walked with Bastian, Angus, Colin and Duncan fell in step with them, emerging together into the clearing where the crumbling cabin stood.

The sheriff exited through the front door, shaking his head. When he spotted Jenna, he moved toward the steps.

"Watch the top step. It's broken," she called out.

The sheriff bypassed the steps and jumped off the porch onto the ground and headed for her, his brow pinched. "I don't know what you think you saw, but the place is completely empty."

CHAPTER 4

JENNA'S BODY froze beneath Bastian's hand. "What do you mean, it's completely empty?" She started forward, stepping out of Bastian's arm. "There was a chair, a battery, jumper cables and rope." She marched to the stairs and started up, passing over the top one to place her foot on the porch.

Bastian hurried to catch up to her. He noted the broken boards and the sagging post at the far end of the porch. He prayed the overhanging awning didn't collapse while they stood beneath it.

Jenna entered the house ahead of him and came to an abrupt standstill in what had been a living area with windows looking out over the back yard.

Like the sheriff said, the room was completely empty.

"I don't understand. The chair was here." She waved her hand at the floor. "There was blood on the floor." Jenna squatted to get closer to the wood planking. Even the blood had been cleaned up. Every last droplet. "It was here."

She stood and faced the sheriff. "Do you have one of those lights? The ones that can illuminate blood that's been cleaned up?" She pointed to the floor. "Look at this floor. If this place had been empty for ten years, it would have a thick layer of dust right here." She walked into the far corner and brushed her foot across the surface, stirring up a puff of dust. "Like this."

The sheriff's eyes narrowed. "As a matter of fact, I do have one of those lights and some Luminol." He left the cabin and was back a moment later with what looked like a flashlight and a small bottle of spray liquid. "Where did you say it was?"

She pointed to a dust-free spot on the floor. "Here."

Sheriff Barron sprayed Luminol on that spot and shined the ultraviolet light over it.

The floor lit up a fluorescent blue in that spot.

Jenna gasped.

Bastian's fists clenched.

There had been blood there.

The sheriff handed the ultraviolet light to Angus to hold as he sprayed more Luminol in a wider radius. Bright blue dots appeared where droplets of blood had been.

Sheriff Barron straightened. "I believe we have a

crime scene." He turned to Jenna. "You say the blood was sticky when you stepped into it?"

She nodded.

"Which means it was fairly fresh." He waved to the McKinnons. "I'll need you all to leave this building, careful not to touch anything. If there's a fingerprint to find, the state crime lab will find it." He touched the button on his radio and called dispatch, requesting a state crime lab evidence collector team ASAP.

Angus nodded to his brothers. "You heard the man. Out."

He herded Colin and Duncan toward the front door.

Jenna looked to Bastian. "I wasn't imagining it."

He shook his head. "No, you weren't." He held out his hand to her.

She laid her fingers in his palm, and he drew her into his embrace. He needed to hold someone. If the blood was his father's, he'd been alive, beaten and tortured.

Jenna wrapped her arms around his waist and pressed her cheek against his chest. "I'm sorry," she whispered.

"For what?" he said, his lips brushing against her temple.

"If it was your father," she murmured, "I'm sorry for what he's having to endure."

"We'll find him and set him free."

"You two need to move on out of here," the sheriff reminded them.

Bastian leaned back. "Ready?"

She nodded.

"Do you have your keys?" he asked.

Jenna dug in her pockets, unearthing the set of keys she'd tucked there so long ago.

He took them from her. "Let's go check out your Jeep."

She frowned up at him. "I didn't even think to look as we drove up. Do you think they might have damaged it?"

"I don't know, but you're not getting into it until we've given it a good once-over." He slipped his arm around her waist and led her toward the door.

Once outside, he crossed over the broken step and helped her descend to the ground. She'd been through so much that day, it was the least he could do.

The Jeep stood several yards from the house.

"When the two men drove up on their motorcycles, they looked at my Jeep."

When Jenna started to reach for the door handle, Bastian grabbed her wrist.

"Let me look it over first," he said.

She frowned and took a step backward. "Okay.

Bastian tried opening the door without using the automatic unlocking mechanism on the key fob. The door opened easily. She'd left it unlocked.

Inside, a purse lay on the floorboard, its contents spewed all over the front seat.

Bastian frowned. "You left the door unlocked and your purse on the seat?"

She nodded. "I was by myself. I didn't expect company. Most people leave their front doors unlocked around here. It used to be a fairly safe community."

He handed her the open wallet. "Look through this and tell me if anything's missing."

She flipped through the credit cards and gasped. "My driver's license. It's not in here." She frowned up at Bastian, her eyes rounding. "They'll know my name."

"And where you live." Bastian's lips pressed together in a thin line. "You can't go back to your place. Do you have someone you can stay with?"

"I'll be fine on my own," she insisted, though her voice wasn't nearly as strong as before he'd reminded her the two men who'd chased her knew where to find her.

"You can't stay alone." He gripped her arms and shook her gently. "You don't know what they'll do."

"They might do nothing. It's not like I saw their faces. They wore helmets, and then ski masks."

"They had to have taken off the helmets for you to see them in ski masks," Bastian said. "They might not know you didn't see them without the helmets. They could think you'll identify them in a lineup."

Jenna's face paled. "Do you really think they would come after me?"

"Yes. I do." He pulled her close, wrapping his arms around her. "You're not safe going back to your place alone. Hell, you're not safe to go to the grocery store alone."

She shook her head, her hands flat against his chest. "I don't know anyone well enough to ask if I can stay the night with them. I don't have many close friends. Just Molly. And my parents moved to Florida." She shrugged. "So, no, I don't have anywhere else to go."

"Then you're coming home to the Iron Horse Ranch."

"I can't impose on you and your family. I already imposed enough when I divorced my husband. I can't do that again."

"My sister and mother will insist on your staying with us."

"Seriously—"

Bastian held up a hand. "I can't stop you from going to your house, but I beg you not to. Please come stay with us until we can figure out who those men were, and if they were involved in what went on in this house." He glanced toward the cabin. "I don't want what happened here to happen to you."

Jenna shivered. "Me either."

"For what it's worth, we second that motion." Angus stepped up beside Bastian. "Mom would be beside herself if we let you go back to your place alone."

Colin raised a hand as if he were swearing in court. "That's the truth."

Duncan nodded.

Jenna glanced from Angus, to Colin, to Duncan and back to Bastian. "Okay. I'll go with you. I'll need to stop at my house to get a few things before I do."

"Before you take off in this Jeep, let us check it over thoroughly," Angus said.

"Exactly what I was going to do," Bastian said.

Colin reached inside the Jeep and popped the hood open. He and Duncan checked the engine, while Bastian and Angus looked beneath the chassis and tested the lights and brakes.

Bastian held the passenger door open for Jenna as she got in. "My bet is they left your Jeep alone. Having cleaned up the evidence, they hoped to discredit you if you brought anyone out here to view a place where someone could have been held hostage."

"Just because we didn't find anything wrong, doesn't mean they didn't tamper with the Jeep," Angus pointed out. "It just means we didn't find anything obvious." He clapped a hand to Bastian's shoulder. "Take it slow and easy back to town in case they tampered with something like the power steering or brakes."

Bastian nodded. "Will do." Then he slid into the

driver's seat, started the engine and drove down the rutted, overgrown driveway and out onto the county-maintained gravel road.

All the way into town, he took many opportunities to test the brakes and power steering. Both appeared to be functioning properly.

When they reached Eagle Rock, Jenna gave him directions to her tiny apartment over the Blue Moose Tavern.

"You live here?"

She nodded. "It's not much, but it's affordable. When I start making more money, I'll buy a house. Until then, at least I know who my neighbors are and, if I need help, there's always someone close."

"At all hours," Bastian said. "Doesn't the noise bother you?"

"I invested in an excellent noise cancelling headset. I sleep quite well." She led the way up to her loft. At her door, Bastian took her key and inserted it into the lock.

He pushed the door inward and felt on the wall for the light switch.

The room lit up with soft white lights shining in the corners and over a narrow bar between the compact living room and the mini kitchen.

He crossed the room to the only other door in the apartment.

"That's just...my bedroom," Jenna said, her voice fading.

"It's the only other place an intruder could hide." He entered her bedroom, checked beneath the bed, in the small closet and the adjoining bathroom. When he was done, he stepped out into the living room. "All clear."

She smiled and shook her head. "Thank you for being so thorough."

He heard the sarcasm in her tone and chose to ignore it. "You're welcome."

Jenna brushed past him and into the bedroom where she pulled a small bag out from beneath the bed and added a pair of jeans, trousers, three sweaters and socks. When she pulled bras and panties out of drawer, Bastian turned away. He walked to the single window overlooking Main Street, his thoughts on the white lace panties and matching bras she'd added to the clothing in the bag.

All day, he'd reminded himself Jenna was his little sister's best friend.

His *little sister*.

Never mind, his sister was a grown woman now and Jenna was, too. He couldn't think about a woman who was his little sister's best friend. That would be like thinking about his sister.

He shot a glance back to the bedroom where he could see Jenna stuffing undergarments into the bag.

She certainly wasn't a little girl anymore, not with full, soft curves in all the right places.

When he'd carried her into the sheriff's office

earlier that day, he'd felt those curves pressed against his body and fought a sudden rise in awareness for this girl who wasn't a girl at all.

He wanted to ask what had happened between her and Corley Ferguson. Why had they divorced, and how long they'd been married? But that would be too personal. Besides, he wasn't interested in starting something with the pretty real estate agent. He was due to go back to active duty once they found his father. And a career as a Navy SEAL didn't make for good family life.

Bastian had made a vow to himself a long time ago that he would never marry. When Lauren had died in that head-on collision all those years ago, he'd felt it was partially his fault she'd died, and he'd lived. If he'd been paying more attention to the traffic in front of him, he might have been able to swerve differently and take the bulk of the impact on his side.

However, the outcome would've been just as deadly. He'd have had to know Lauren had skipped engaging her seatbelt. The head-on collision had been unavoidable. The only thing that would have changed the outcome, was if he'd noticed her lack of a seatbelt and insisted she buckle up. With hindsight being twenty-twenty and the past being unchangeable, he couldn't bring Lauren back to life, or alter history.

"I'm ready," Jenna said from the door of her

bedroom. She carried a soft-sided bag in one hand and a tote in the other. She'd changed out of the dirty clothes, brushed the tangles and twigs from her hair and washed the dirt and makeup from her face.

If anything, she looked even more desirable. Her face, clean of makeup, emphasized the natural pink of her lips.

A sudden urge to taste those lips washed over Bastian. He took a step toward her and stopped.

What was he thinking?

For a moment, he closed his eyes to the beauty in front of him. Then he squared his shoulders, opened his eyes and took the larger bag from her hand. "It's getting late. My mother will be waiting dinner for our arrival."

"She shouldn't wait on us."

"You'll be her guest. Of course, she should."

Jenna smiled. "That's sweet of her, but not necessary. I spent so much of my childhood in your mother's house, I felt like one of the family."

Exactly the reason why he couldn't have sexy thoughts about her. She was like a sister.

Then why did he want to kiss her like she wasn't?

Bastian was first out the door and down the steps as if he was being chased by the hounds of hell.

"Hey, are you forgetting something?" Jenna called out from the top of the stairs.

He turned, a frown pulling his eyebrows together. "Am I?"

She rolled her eyes. "For a moment there, I thought you'd load up my bags and leave without me." Jenna hurried down the stairs and caught up with him.

They fell in step beside each other.

"My apologies," he muttered.

"Something bothering you?" she asked.

If only she knew how loaded that question was. "No," he said and tossed her bag on the back seat of her vehicle.

Jenna laid her tote on the back floorboard and climbed into the front passenger seat.

Bastian closed the door and rounded the vehicle to the other side, sliding into the driver's seat.

Jenna turned to him. "If it bothers you for me to stay at Iron Horse Ranch, I would just as soon stay in my own apartment."

"It would bother me more if you stayed here." He shifted into gear and pulled out of the parking lot.

"Then why are you frowning?"

He drew in a deep breath and let it go. "I have a lot on my mind."

Jenna touched his arm, sending a spark of electricity throughout his body. "I'm sorry. It makes me sick to my stomach thinking about whoever was tortured in that cabin. I hope it wasn't your father."

"And in a strange way, I hope it was. It means he's still alive and somewhere nearby." Bastian balled his fist and tapped the steering wheel with it. "We just have to find him."

"Soon," Jenna added quietly.

Bastian nodded. "You say the men who chased you carried military grade weapons?"

"Yes. They looked like the ones that deployed soldiers carry. Their clothing looked like something you'd wear into combat, with pockets and loops to carry ammunition. Instead of camouflage, the fabric was all black, including the ski masks.

"Do you know of any para-military organizations training in the area?"

Jenna shook her head. "I know we have preppers or survivalists, but I wasn't aware of any that were training like a military organization or purchasing military arms."

"I'll have my friend Hank Patterson look into it. Maybe he can discover who out here might own semi-automatic rifles."

"And why they would feel the need to do what they were doing in the cabin." Jenna twisted her hands in her lap. "It's hard to believe stuff like that is happening in our own backyard."

"There are some sadistic bastards in the world. And they aren't all confined to war zones."

When they pulled up to the house on Iron Horse Ranch, Bastian's mother and his sister Molly were the first out the door and down the steps to greet Jenna.

"Jenna," his mother cried. "We heard what happened to you." She pulled her into her arms and hugged her hard. "I feel like my second daughter just came home," she said, wiping a tear from the corner of her eye.

"I hope I won't be an inconvenience to you." Jenna leaned back and gave Bastian's mother a weak smile. "I could have stayed in town."

"No way." Molly moved in for the second hug. "It'll be like a sleepover, only longer. I can't remember the last time we had a slumber party."

"Graduation from high school," Bastian's mother said. "You and your five other friends stayed up all night long, playing music, singing karaoke and lying beneath the stars, planning your lives."

Jenna snorted. "So much for those plans."

"But you're here now." Hannah McKinnon took Jenna's hand. "Dinner first."

"I should carry my things up to my room first."

"Let Molly and Bastian do that. You must be exhausted. I heard all about your terrible ordeal from Angus. But I'd like to hear it from you, if you're okay talking about it." She led Jenna toward the dining room.

Molly chuckled. "Mom knows how to make someone feel at home." She glanced up at Bastian. "Thank you for making her come. I tried for years to get her to stay out here."

"Why?"

Molly tipped her head. "You didn't know?"

"Know what?"

"That rat-bastard, ex-husband of hers, Corley Ferguson, used to beat the crap out of her. She tried to hide it, but everyone knew. You can't hide black eyes and bruised cheeks. I told her to leave him so many times, I lost count." Molly lifted the tote bag Jenna had laid on the floor by the door. "You want me to take that duffel?"

Bastian stared at the door Jenna had gone through with his mother. "No. I've got it. Lead the way." He followed his sister up the stairs, wanting to learn more about Jenna's life between the time he'd left home and now. "What made her finally divorce him?"

"He nearly killed her. After he left her on the floor in their house with three broken ribs and a concussion, she called 911. She hasn't been back since."

"How long ago was that?"

Molly shrugged. "The divorce was final a year ago. She had to file for a restraining order after he'd cornered her at her work. It had been her first day on the job as a real estate agent." At the top of the stairs, Molly turned left and stopped in front of the room beside Bastian's.

"Did he hurt her again?" Bastian asked.

Molly grinned. "Hell no. Jenna and I spent the summer driving back and forth to Bozeman to take Krav Maga self-defense lessons. She whooped ol' Corley's ass." Molly shook her head. "I would have given good money to see that bastard on his knees." Her lips pressed into a firm line. "He deserved it and a whole lot more."

"Has he kept his distance since the restraining order?"

"As far as I know. I haven't heard of anymore incidents. Jenna seems to be getting on with her life. Hopefully, Corley is, too." She set the tote on the bed. "I'm glad she's here for a while. I worried about her living over the Blue Moose."

"Why did she stay there?"

"She's trying to build up her sales as a real estate agent. It takes time. She didn't ask for anything out of her divorce from Corley. She just wanted to be free of the abuse. But she's flat broke, living from one sale to another."

Bastian's chest pinched at the thought of Jenna going hungry until she saw another paycheck. Especially, when the McKinnons had so much.

He set the soft-sided duffel bag on the bed beside the tote and followed Molly out of the room.

Bastian was glad Jenna was staying at the ranch as well. No woman deserved to be beaten like Corley had beaten her. Only cowards and bullies hit women. As far as Bastian was concerned, those men didn't need to occupy space on the planet.

He hurried downstairs, this newfound understanding of Jenna making him anxious to see her again. After being abused so violently and then chased through the woods by para-military assassins, she was holding up better than most women in similar situations. One more reason for him to admire his sister's best friend.

Admire...but don't touch, he reminded himself.

Admiration could get him in trouble. That, combined with the desire to kiss her, sent up red flags for Bastian. He'd never wanted to be responsible for another woman after Lauren. And he hadn't been tempted for the past eleven years.

Until now. Until Jenna.

CHAPTER 5

JENNA WOKE with a start and stared up at the ceiling. She didn't recognize the room or the furniture. Panic seized her until she realized she wasn't tied to a wooden chair, nor was she in a dark, dingy old cabin awaiting torture.

She sat up straight and rubbed her wrists. Her heart hammered against her ribs until she remembered. This wasn't her apartment over the Blue Moose Tavern. She'd stayed the night with the McKinnons on the Iron Horse Ranch. If she wasn't safe here, she wasn't safe anywhere.

She laid back on the pillow and willed herself to sleep. After several minutes lying with her eyes squeezed shut, she finally gave up, sat up and swung her legs over the side of the bed.

Five o'clock in the morning wasn't too early to rise, was it? Jenna dressed and carried her boots down the stairs where a light burned brightly from the kitchen.

The aroma of coffee filled the air, leading her in the direction of the kitchen, the coffee pot and company.

Molly's mother, Hannah McKinnon, dressed in jeans, a white blouse and house slippers, stood at the coffeemaker pouring a cup of the fragrant brew into a mug. When she turned, she smiled. "I don't remember...do you drink coffee?"

Jenna nodded. "Yes, ma'am."

"Oh, please, don't call me ma'am."

"Yes, Mrs. McKinnon."

"And that sounds too formal for us adults. Why don't you call me Mom? After all, you're like one of mine." She held out the cup. "There's cream in the refrigerator and sugar on the table."

"Thanks, but I like it just like this." Jenna closed her eyes and inhaled. Something about the scent of a good cup of coffee grounded her in the day.

"I expect the men will be up soon. I heard Angus on the phone with Hank Patterson late last night. He said Hank and his computer guy will be out first thing this morning."

Jenna's eyebrows rose. "They get up at five o'clock?"

"Is it only five?" Mrs. McKinnon shot a glance toward the clock on the wall and grimaced. "I guess they won't be out here that soon." She poured a cup and carried it to the table where she sat.

"Why are you up so early?" Jenna asked as she took a seat opposite of the McKinnon matriarch.

Hannah sighed. "I couldn't sleep."

"Missing James?"

The older woman nodded, her eyes suspiciously glassy. "The bed is so big without him. And lonely." She glanced toward the window, the cup of coffee in her hands all but forgotten. "I can only imagine what he must be going through, and it tears me up." She set the cup on the table, pulled a tissue out of her front pocket and dabbed at her eyes. "There I go again. You'd think I couldn't handle a little adversity."

Jenna set down her cup and reached across the table to grip Hannah's empty hand. "You have a right to be upset. It's frustrating when you have no control over the situation."

"If only I could do something. Anything. But all I've done is wait." Hannah shook her head. "I'm tired of waiting. I need action."

"We all do," Bastian's voice sounded from behind Jenna.

Jenna spun, heat rising up her neck into her cheeks. She pressed a hand to her chest. "Don't do that."

He grinned. "Do what?"

"Sneak up on a person."

He frowned. "I'm sorry if I frightened you."

She drew in a deep breath and let it out. "I'm all right."

His mother pushed back her chair and started to rise.

"Sit," he said, waving at her. "I know how to pour a cup of coffee."

She rose anyway. "I should start breakfast. I'm sure the others will be down soon."

Bastian placed a hand on her shoulder. "Mom, no one will be down for another hour at least. Sit and relax."

She gave him a tight smile. "I need to move."

Jenna caught Bastian's gaze and gave him a brief nod. "When you're upset or worried about something or someone, it helps to keep busy."

Mrs. McKinnon nodded. "Exactly. If I sit too long, my mind goes down dark paths. I need to remain positive. Therefore, I can't sit long." She covered Bastian's hand on her shoulder. "I love you son, but you gotta let me do my thing."

He pulled her into a brief hug. "Gotcha. You do your thing."

"Are you hungry yet?" she asked as she crossed the floor. "Or can you wait while I whip up a batch of homemade biscuits?"

He grinned. "I can wait as long as it takes for your homemade biscuits."

"They're your dad's favorites. Maybe, if I make

them, he'll smell them and find his way home." She laughed, the sound catching on a sob.

"Makes sense to me. I know he'd come home, if he could." Bastian poured a cup of coffee and leaned against the counter to drink it. "Anything I can do to help?"

His mother snorted. "Have you ever made biscuits in your entire life?"

"No, but I can reach stuff in tall cabinets," he said. "That ought to be worth something." He winked at Jenna and smiled at his mother.

Jenna's heart skipped several beats. Bastian had never winked at her before. Still, she shouldn't read anything into it. He didn't see her as anyone but his kid sister's friend.

As Jenna finished her coffee, she too felt the need to move. "Can I help?" she asked.

Mrs. McKinnon shook her head. "Not until I start cooking the eggs and bacon to go with the biscuits. I could use some fresh eggs. I think the stash in the refrigerator is low."

"I'll check the chicken coop," Jenna said. She and Molly used to collect the eggs when they'd been teens.

"Watch out for the rooster. Lately, he's been a cantankerous little cuss. Use the fishnet hanging on the barn if he acts like he's going to attack you."

"Fish net?" Bastian frowned. "What do you mean?"

"I know what she's talking about," Jenna said with a grin. "I'll handle it."

"I've got to see this. Who uses a fishnet to collect eggs?"

Jenna's nerves all stood on alert as she led the way out to the chicken coop.

Just as Mrs. McKinnon had predicted, as soon as they opened the gate to the chicken pen, the rooster rushed at them, wings flapping.

Having been spurred by a rooster before, Jenna wasn't going to put up with his nonsense or suffer the puncture wounds his sharp talons could induce. She closed the gate, grabbed the fishnet hanging on a nail on the outside of the barn and returned to the chicken pen. "Watch and learn," she said to Bastian.

Jenna opened the gate.

When the rooster charged, she scooped him up into the fishnet. She hung the net, rooster and all, on the nail sticking out of the side of the chicken coop and collected the eggs with no more problems.

Bastian stood at the gate, his arms crossed, a smile tugging at the corners of his lips. "Clever."

"Your mother figured it out a long time ago. I learned from the best." She handed him the bucket of eggs. "If you'll hold this, I'll release our prisoner."

"I'll take care of the rooster."

Jenna stepped back and let him.

Soon the disgruntled rooster was once again strutting his stuff among the hens in the chicken yard. And Jenna had a bucket of fresh eggs for breakfast.

Bastian shook his head. "My mother…"

"Is brilliant. I never would have thought to hang the rooster on the wall so that I could collect eggs."

"You enjoyed that, didn't you?" He took the bucket from her hands and carried it to the house.

"I did. It's been a long time since I've been out here. Other than when I stayed here after my divorce."

"I thought you and Molly would have kept in touch after high school. Eagle Rock isn't that big a town."

Jenna's smile slipped. "I was busy."

"What did you do before you sold real estate?" he asked.

She didn't want to answer, but she didn't want the easy way he was talking to her to end. "Not much."

"Did you work outside the home when you were married to Ferguson?"

"No," she responded. Thankfully, they arrived at the back door. Jenna dove into the kitchen and called out brightly, "We have eggs."

"Oh, good," Mrs. McKinnon said. "Just in time. Hank and Swede just drove up, and the biscuits are almost ready." She took the bucket from her son and carried them to the stove.

Within minutes, she had a dozen eggs cracked, stirred and poured into a skillet to scramble.

Unwilling to answer more questions from Bastian, Jenna made herself useful by popping bread into the toaster and buttering them when they were done.

"Bastian, I need you to set the table," Mrs. McKinnon said.

Angus, Colin and Molly entered the room, followed by two men Jenna had seen in Eagle Rock on several occasions, but had never been properly introduced to.

Duncan and Parker Bailey, the ranch foreman, followed the strangers into the kitchen.

"Mom," Angus said. "You've met Hank and Swede."

"Yes, of course. They've been a big help with the investigation to find your father." Mrs. McKinnon raised a spatula. "I hope you like scrambled eggs and biscuits."

"Yes, ma'am," Hank answered. "But you don't have to feed us."

"Don't be silly. It's early. I'm sure you haven't had time to grab breakfast. And it won't be any trouble to add a few more eggs."

"Thank you, ma'am," the men said.

Bastian held out a hand to the dark-haired man. "Hank." He motioned to Jenna. "This is Jenna Meyers, the woman who discovered the blood in the cabin yesterday. Jenna, this is Hank Patterson, founder of the Brotherhood Protectors, a security and protection service made up of prior military soldiers, sailors and marines."

Hank held out his hand to Jenna. "I hear you had a little trouble yesterday with some men carrying military-grade weapons. I'm glad you were able to evade them and report back to the sheriff, without any undo harm."

"It's a pleasure to meet you, Mr. Patterson," she said, shaking his hand. "I didn't realize we needed so much private security in this area, but I'm glad you're here."

"Call me Hank." He turned to a hulkingly big man with pale blond hair. "This is Swede. He's my right hand and tech guru. We couldn't do half the things we do without his guidance and support."

Jenna shook Swede's big hand and looked up into friendly blue eyes. Despite his intimidating size, she liked him instantly.

Hank turned to the McKinnon men. "I was able to scrape up some of the blood samples off the cabin floor. Since the state crime lab is always backed up and takes too incredibly long to run identification testing, I offered to send it to a lab I know of where they can perform DNA testing in a fraction of the time."

"Thank you," Angus said.

"Yes," Mrs. McKinnon. "Thank you."

Hank held up his hands. "If you want to know if the blood was Mr. McKinnon's, I'll need something of his that would contain his DNA. A hair would be ideal."

Mrs. McKinnon nodded her head. "I can do that. I know where he kept his favorite comb. Hopefully, it has enough hair on it to make the DNA testing a possibility." She handed the spatula to Colin. "Stir the scrambled eggs to keep them from sticking to the bottom."

Colin nodded. "Don't worry, I've made scrambled eggs before."

"Now, I'm really scared." Mrs. McKinnon took the spatula from Colin and handed it to Duncan. "Keep your eye on the ball. If you don't keep stirring, they'll burn to the bottom of the pan."

"Go," Duncan said. "I've got this."

Hannah McKinnon hurried out of the room, her slippered feet slapping on the stairs as she climbed to the second floor.

Colin stood beside Duncan. "You're burning the eggs."

"No, I'm not," Duncan said, wielding the spatula like he knew what he was doing.

Jenna liked the playful bickering between the brothers. The love and warmth in the room made her feel safe.

"Mind if I get a cup of that coffee?" Hank asked.

"Not at all," Angus said. "Make yourself at home." He pulled two mugs out of the cabinet over the coffeemaker and set them beside the carafe.

"Cream is in the refrigerator, and the sugar is on the table."

Hank poured a cup for Swede and one for himself and sat at the table. "I spoke to the sheriff this morning. They're questioning local survivalist groups about the two men on motorcycles."

"I'm certain they won't hand over their two men if they were involved in the abduction and torture," Bastian said.

"Still, the sheriff will poke around and see what he can," Hank said. "In the meantime, I'll send some of my guys to stake out their camps. If we see anything, we'll report back."

Bastian glanced across at Jenna. "I'd like to talk with your mountain man. If he's living in the woods, he might be seeing things the rest of us aren't."

Jenna's lips twisted. "Even if you can find him, he won't talk."

"What do you mean," Bastian asked.

She shrugged. "He communicated with me in hand signals."

"I don't care if he talks, as long as he can lead me to anything related to our father," Bastian said.

"I'm all for that, too," Jenna said. "However, I think it'll be hard to get him to do anything he doesn't want to do. He knows how to disappear."

His jaw firm, Bastian tapped his fist into his open palm. "I'll find him."

"I'm going with you," Jenna said.

Bastian's brow dipped. "You should stay here at the ranch where you're safe. Those men know you saw something."

Molly entered the kitchen with her mother "Jenna, Bastian has a point. Those men chased you through the woods. I don't think they were carrying rifles to make sure you said yes to having tea with them."

Jenna's lips quirked at Molly's sarcasm. The mental image of the dangerous men having tea struck her as hysterically funny. Key word: hysterically.

She squared her shoulders and set her mouth in a firm line. "I'm not going to hide out on the Iron Horse Ranch forever. I have a life. I refuse to run scared...ever again."

"Jenna," Bastian said. "There's a difference between running scared and being cautious."

"I know." She lifted her chin. "I also know my mountain man is skittish. He might not let you get close. He saved my life. I have a better chance of coaxing him out of hiding. Assuming we can find him in the first place." She frowned. "I meant to ask the sheriff if he knew of such a man, but we were all so caught up in getting back to the cabin, I forgot."

"Our first stop today will be to talk to Sheriff Barron."

"Then I'm going with you...?" Jenna asked.

"Although it's against my better judgement," Bastian said. "Yes."

Molly hugged Jenna. "I'm all for you going with my big brother, but promise me you'll be safe."

Jenna's heart swelled as she hugged her friend. "I will."

"I'm glad we have that settled." Mrs. McKinnon held out two paper bags. "Hank, here's my husband's comb. I believe there are a few hairs on it. And his razor. The hairs are smaller, but there are some there. I'd like to have those back when you're done with them. Those are his favorites, and he'll need them when he comes home."

"I'll get these to the DNA lab and back to you as soon as possible," Hank promised.

"And before you all bug out, you'll sit and have a decent breakfast," Mrs. McKinnon commanded as only a matriarch of a mostly male family could. "Who knows when you'll eat again?"

Duncan set a huge bowl of fluffy yellow scrambled eggs in the middle of the table.

Mrs. McKinnon set a basket of fresh, hot biscuits beside the bowl and a plate of crisp bacon.

Molly, Bastian and Angus hurried to pour juice into glasses and refill coffee mugs.

Soon, they all sat around the table.

"If you don't mind, I'd like to say a prayer," Mrs. McKinnon said.

They joined hands and bowed their heads.

"Dear Lord, please guide these young men and women to my husband and keep them safe in the process. That's all I ask. Amen."

"Amen," Jenna said along with the rest of the people at the table. A long pause followed.

"Eat," Mrs. McKinnon said and passed the bowl of scrambled eggs to Angus.

They consumed the meal quickly, talking over their plans for the day.

Jenna sat in silence, pushing her eggs around on the plate. If she were honest with herself, she was a little scared about going back out into the mountains.

After the beating she took from Corley, she'd promised herself never to be scared again. Taking control of the situation was what had brought her out of the corner she'd painted her life into.

What had happened yesterday took "out of control" to an entirely different level.

Men with military weapons? She couldn't stand up to that, not without intensive combat training and more fire power than her .40 caliber handgun.

When the others finished their meals, they carried their empty plates to the sink.

Jenna carried hers to the counter. "Is there a container I can save this in?" she asked Mrs. McKinnon.

The older woman slipped an arm around her waist. "Are you feeling okay?"

"Yes," Jenna lied. "I wasn't as hungry as I thought I was." She gave her a weak smile.

"Bastian will take good care of you. He won't take you into an unsafe situation."

"I know that." She sighed. "But what if I take him into an unsafe situation?"

"He's a Navy SEAL," his mother said, her chest puffing out. "He's used to that. He can handle a lot more than the average guy."

Bastian turned. "What are you ladies plotting? Do I need to be afraid?"

"Not at all." Mrs. McKinnon laid a plastic container on the counter. "We were just discussing the weather."

Bastian's eyes narrowed as his gaze captured Jenna's. "It's supposed to be partly cloudy and cool. You might want to bring a warm jacket."

Jenna's cheeks flamed as she scraped her eggs into the container. "I'll be ready to go in less than five minutes." She snapped the top onto the container, shoved it into the refrigerator and darted for the stairs.

In her room, she slipped her shoulder holster over her arms, buckled it in place and dragged a warm jacket over it. She didn't bother with makeup, but she dragged a brush through her hair and pulled it back into a ponytail with a thin, elastic band.

As satisfied with her appearance as she could be for a potential tromp through the woods, she left the room and descended to the foyer where Bastian waited by the door, talking with Hank, Swede and Angus.

"Are you sure you don't want us to go with you to find this mountain man?" Hank asked.

"I think the more people the less likely we'll even get near him. It might even be better if I go in alone," she said.

"No," Bastian said without hesitation, his eyes steely and his jaw set in stone. "You're not going anywhere alone."

Jenna stiffened. "You're not my keeper."

He remained unbending for another second, maybe two. Then his shoulders loosened, and his mouth twisted. "You're right. I'd prefer if you didn't go alone. I'm used to operating as a team, even when the team consists of only two people. Everybody needs someone who has his six."

"Six?" Jenna frowned.

He jerked a thumb over his shoulder. "Twelve o'clock is the direction you face. Six is behind you. You don't have eyes in the back of your head, so you need someone guarding your six."

Jenna nodded. "I get it. Okay. I'll let you have my six. But it goes both ways."

When he looked like he might argue the point, she raised an eyebrow. "You think I won't be of any use?"

"I didn't say that."

"I've trained with my handgun. I'm licensed to

carry a concealed weapon." She waved open her jacket. "And I'm not afraid to use it."

"Why didn't you use it when the men with the rifles were after you?" Angus asked.

"There were two of them and one of me. I didn't know if they meant harm. Even if I had fired on them, no matter how good I am on the range, they were moving. If I missed, I'd only have a short amount of time to aim again and get it right. I thought it more prudent to lie low and hide. I'd have shot them if they came closer and threatened me."

Bastian nodded. "Fair enough. I'll have your back."

"And I'll have yours." She stepped through the door. "First stop, sheriff's office?"

"Yes." Bastian led the way to his truck.

"Why not my vehicle?"

"If your military-rifle-bearing guys are looking for you, they'll find you sooner if you drive your Jeep. They won't expect to find you in my truck."

"Fair enough." Her lips twitched at the corners as she climbed into the passenger seat.

All those years she'd had a secret crush on Molly's older brother, and he hadn't noticed that she existed. Now, eleven years later, he was insisting she stick with him like glue. Her younger heart would have fluttered at the intimacy of riding beside him in his truck.

Her mature heart wasn't much different.

She hoped they could find her mountain man,

and that he had more information about the cabin, the men who'd chased them and the whereabouts of James McKinnon.

In the meantime, Jenna enjoyed being in the same vehicle as the man she'd fantasized about marrying one day.

CHAPTER 6

Bastian didn't like the idea of Jenna traipsing all over the county looking for a mysterious mountain man. She'd made herself a target by exploring the cabin in the woods. Shouldn't she be lying low until they found the men responsible for the torture room?

He bit back his frustration and drove toward Eagle Rock.

"Sheriff's office?" Jenna asked.

"I thought we'd start there. He might know who your mountain man is."

"If not, he'll know who to ask," Jenna added.

Bastian parked in front of the sheriff's office and got out.

Jenna was down from her seat before he could get around to her side to open the door for her. Another reason to be slightly perturbed. But he held back any comments. The woman had a mind of her own. After living in an abusive relationship, she might not want a man to say or do anything that breathed of control.

He couldn't blame her for the attitude. Corley Ferguson had better steer clear of them while Bastian was in town. He wouldn't put up with the bastard's wife-beating ways.

Inside, Jenna addressed the man at the counter. "We'd like to speak with Sheriff Barron."

"The sheriff's in his office," the officer on the front desk said. "He's on the phone." The man glanced down at the phone on his desk. "He just hung up."

The sheriff poked his head out of his office. "I thought I heard you two come in. Please, come in."

Jenna led the way with Bastian following close behind.

Once inside the sheriff's office, Jenna spoke. "Sir, do you know who my mountain man from yesterday might be? I meant to ask yesterday, but we were all busy checking out the cabin, and I forgot."

The sheriff nodded. "Yesterday was insanely busy. And today is no different. The state crime lab sent out a team to process the evidence at the cabin. In a few minutes, I'll be on my way out there." He frowned. "I've been thinking about what you said about the man who hid you from the two guys on the motorcycles. I think I know who that might be."

Jenna smiled. "Great. And if you know where we can find him, that would be even better."

Sheriff Barron shook his head. "I have a couple of ideas of where to find him, but no guarantees."

He glanced out the window to the gray, cloudy morning. "There was a man who'd lost his wife in a snowstorm some eight years ago. They were on their way back from Bozeman when it hit. He pulled over to the side of the road because he couldn't see well enough to drive." The sheriff looked back at Jenna. "The snow completely covered their truck. It was early fall. They weren't expecting a snowstorm, so they didn't have the usual survival items on hand. No blanket, no candles or matches. All they had were the jackets they wore when they set out to Bozeman early that morning."

"You never know what kind of crazy Montana weather is going to strike," Bastian said.

"Exactly," the sheriff agreed. "Long story short, the snow continued, it got colder, the temperature dropping to below zero. He decided he had to get help, or his wife would freeze to death."

"I can guess where this is going," Jenna said, saddened by the story.

The sheriff nodded. "He left the truck and started walking along the highway toward Eagle Rock, praying he would find someone along the way who could help. Several hours later, he made it to Eagle Rock. He and one of the local tow truck owners headed back down the highway to rescue his wife."

Jenna pressed her fingers to her lips, her eyes rounding.

"They couldn't find the car. The wind was blowing hard. The blowing snow had covered his tracks and...he couldn't find the car."

Bastian's heart squeezed hard in his chest.

"Oh my god." Jenna's eyes filled. "That's horrible."

"They searched for hours. When they finally stumbled across a certain snow drift, they found it. But it was too late." The sheriff shook his head. "His wife had died of exposure."

"You think my mountain man was the husband?" Jenna whispered.

Sheriff Barron nodded. "Earl Monson. His wife was Vera Monson. They'd been together for over forty years. Earl must be in his late sixties. He left the house they'd built together and disappeared into the mountains."

"Do you know where we might find him?" Bastian asked.

"Not exactly," the sheriff said with a frown. "Hunters have spotted him on occasion in various hunting cabins or near caves. He's come into town to trade carvings for cash to buy staples at the grocery store. Then he disappears again."

"How does he survive?" Jenna asked.

"I don't know. After eight years, I'm sure he's gotten good at living off the land," Sheriff Barron said. "I can give you the general locations of the places he's most likely to be, considering he was close to the Mahon cabin. You'll need a four-wheeler or horse to get back in there. The roads aren't going to get you there easily."

"We have access to four-wheelers," Bastian said.

"Good." The sheriff pulled up a contour map of the area surrounding the Mahon property and pointed to a nearby ridge. "There's a hunting cabin on the east side of this ridge. I know, because I hunted back there in my younger days. It's the closest to the Mahon cabin. If he's not there..." The sheriff pointed to a narrow valley on the other side of the ridge. "There's another really small cabin on the other side of the ridge. It's more of a hut than a cabin. It's also within reasonable walking distance of the Mahon cabin."

"What about closer to town?" Jenna asked. "He walked me to a trail that led into town. Are there other cabins closer to town?"

The sheriff nodded. "There are a couple, but they're used more frequently by locals. I doubt he'd be there. If he isn't at one of the first two I showed you, try the ones closer to town." He printed out the contour map and handed it to Bastian. "Good luck. And while you're out there, beware of survivalist camps. They're out there, and they move often to avoid detection."

Bastian nodded. "Will do."

As they climbed into the truck and headed back

to the Iron Horse Ranch, Bastian was quiet, trying to decide which way he wanted to get into the hills to find Earl Monson.

"We need to go in on horseback," Jenna said. "It's the only way to get in there without making a lot of noise way in advance of arriving at our destination."

He glanced her way. "I was just thinking the same thing." His brow dipped. "Are you up to riding?"

"About as much as you are," she said. "We haven't been on horseback in a while. I'm sure we'll be sore, but I don't see any other way to get in there without him hearing us from way off. We almost need to sneak up on Earl so that he doesn't have time to bolt."

"Agreed." Bastian pulled into the ranch and around to the barn where he backed up to the horse trailer.

Molly and Parker came out of the barn wearing gloves and carrying rakes.

"Whatcha doing?" Molly asked.

"Taking a couple of horses out to find Jenna's mountain man," Bastian said.

Molly nodded. "You'll want Little Joe, and Jenna can ride Scout."

"I'll bring Little Joe in from the field," Parker said.

"And Scout is in his stall," Molly said. "Let's get him saddled before you load him on the trailer."

Jenna helped Molly saddle Scout.

Parker led Little Joe in from the field and saddled the gelding.

By that time, Bastian had the trailer hooked up and pulled up to the hitch on his truck. He pulled around to the front of the barn and opened the back door.

Molly led Scout in and tied his bridle to a loop on the wall. She backed out of the trailer and Parker led Little Joe in behind Scout.

Once the horses were settled, Bastian closed the trailer door. "Ready?" he asked

Jenna nodded.

"All you have to do is say the word," Molly said with a smile. "And I'll go with you."

Jenna hugged her friend. "Thanks. I think fewer is better. We can move in quietly and hope to see him before he sees us."

"Are you sure you'll be safe?" Parker asked.

Bastian worried about the same thing. "We hope so."

"Why don't we come along?" Molly said, raising her hand as Jenna opened her mouth to protest. "We can stay with the truck and trailer. You can take some hand-held radios and call if you need us to come in for backup."

Bastian nodded. "Not a bad idea."

"Really?" Molly grinned. "I'll grab the radios." She ducked into the tack room and was out again in a couple of seconds, carrying a few two-way radios.

"Where's Colin, Duncan and Angus?" Bastian asked.

"They headed to town to ask about gun sales at the feed store," Parker said.

"And Mom?"

"I think she's on a cleaning binge," Molly said, shaking her head. "Something about having to stay busy. I offered to help, but she declined. Fiona's leaving baby Caity with Mom after lunch, while Fiona does some grocery shopping."

Bastian grinned. "Caity will keep her plenty busy."

Finding out she had a granddaughter had helped his mother through the trying days since her husband had been missing. Little Caity was the bright spot in her day.

His brother Duncan hadn't known he had a daughter until he'd come home on leave to help find his father. At least some good things had come of the whole sad situation. Duncan, Fiona and Caity would become the family they were meant to be.

It had been good for Angus and Colin as well. Angus had reconnected with his high school sweetheart, Bree, and Colin had reunited with his best friend from high school, Emily.

Bastian would not have that luxury. His high school sweetheart was dead. There would be no reunion love story for him. Not that he wanted one. As a Navy SEAL, he was married to his job. He could be called to duty at a moment's notice and disappear for months at a time. That kind of work wasn't something that made for good family life.

He'd seen too many of his buddies divorce after the first year of marriage. Those whose relationships lasted long enough to have children, missed all the firsts. First steps, first day at school, first ball game, first date.

His gaze shifted to Jenna. She was like a phoenix. She'd risen out of a bad situation and became stronger. Now, she valued her independence and the fact she could stand on her own two feet. She didn't need a man in her life.

That's the kind of woman who could hack being a Navy SEAL's wife. She wouldn't need to have a man around fulltime.

He bet, with the right man, a man who treated her with love and respect, she'd learn to trust again.

If she were his wife, he'd show her that a man could be gentle and considerate. Not all men were animals like Corley Ferguson.

If Jenna were his wife...

What was he thinking? She was his kid sister's friend.

All grown up, but still...

He glanced at Parker, holding open the door to the truck's back seat for Molly. He smiled as he handed her up into the seat. Why was he grinning at her like she was some sexy morsel?

His little sister wasn't little anymore. She was a grown woman.

Bastian's gaze switched back to Jenna, who was

rounding the truck to the passenger side. She didn't have to be his wife for him to show her that chivalry wasn't dead. He treated all women with care and concern, when he wasn't standing around ruminating about the past and everything he couldn't fix in the world. Why the hell wasn't he opening her door for her?

"Let me get that," He hurried around and pulled the door open.

"I'm perfectly capable of opening my own doors," she said.

He found himself smiling at her like Parker had smiled at Molly. "I know you are. But my mother taught me to be better. She taught me to open doors for old ladies at a very young age."

Jenna paused with her foot on the running board and cocked an eyebrow. "So, are you telling me I'm an old woman, now?"

He back-paddled. "No, of course not. But you're...older."

"Older than what?" She shook her head. "Older than dirt?"

"No, no." He ran a hand through his hair. Where had he gone wrong? He'd only wanted to make her feel special by opening the door for her.

"Quit while you're ahead, Bastian," Parker said. "Some battles you just have to walk away from."

"Oh, hell." Bastian gripped Jenna around the waist, lifted her up into her seat and closed the door.

He stomped around to the other side, got in and started the engine. Before he shifted into gear, he turned to Jenna. "For the record, I don't think you're old. On the contrary, you're young, beautiful and I admire your courage and spunk. Now, can we get on with this mission before I shoot myself in the foot again?"

Molly and Parker laughed out loud in the back seat.

Bastian gripped the gear shift and shoved it into drive. That's what he got for trying to be nice.

A hand covered his on the shift knob.

He looked toward Jenna. Their gazes locked.

"Thank you," she said. No sarcasm, no derision, just sincerity and a gentle smile.

But there was nothing gentle about the way her touch made his blood slam through his veins. He liked that she'd touched him. Liked it a bit too much.

Focus, frogman.

He eased the truck and trailer out of the barnyard, down the driveway and out onto the highway. They had a job to do, a mission to accomplish. He couldn't be thinking about kissing a girl when his father was still missing. Not to mention, they were about to go horseback riding in the mountains where they could potentially run into heavily armed men who might feel like Jenna knew too much to let her roam free.

Yeah, he'd be better off focusing on the road ahead and the situation at hand, not the hand on his arm that made him want to park the truck and pull her into his arms.

JENNA HAD FELT a rush of electricity blast through her system when she'd laid her hand on Bastian's arm. She'd always had a thing for him as a young teen, but what she felt now was quite different. This wasn't the school-aged crush of a fourteen-year-old.

Being with Bastian made heat coil low in her belly. Her pulse quickened and desire washed over her like a tidal wave. She hadn't felt that kind of desire for a long time. No. She'd never felt that level of intensity. Ever. Not when she had a crush on him. Not when she'd dated and married Corley.

What had just happened was different. It was a rush of excitement, a burning sensation that spread throughout her body and made her want to rip her clothes off and make love to Bastian in broad daylight.

Wow.

She sat in her seat, staring out at the road ahead, afraid to look at Bastian in case he saw what she was feeling. It was so strong, she was sure it would be evident in her eyes. Or maybe she was overreacting. How could anybody be that turned on by just laying a hand on a man's arm?

And what happened to her vow to remain abstinent and free of all men? Hadn't she thought they were all sex-hungry control freaks?

She knew that was painting all men with the same brush, but after what Corley had done to her, she'd been afraid of trusting any man.

Thankfully, she was beginning to understand that not all men were complete bastards like Corley. Each of the McKinnon brothers and Parker, their foreman, had been nothing but kind to her.

After Corley had beaten her so badly, the counselor she'd seen said that she would probably suffer PTSD from the trauma. She'd handled it by swearing off dating. Besides, she was sure that, if she tried to date, Corley would have something to say about it and violate the restraining order. Not many men would want to step into a relationship with a woman whose ex-husband was prone to violence.

She dared to look at Bastian. He was a man who wouldn't be afraid of Corley. And Corley wouldn't stand a chance in a fight with this McKinnon, or any of the McKinnons, for that matter.

Jenna felt better knowing she could take care of herself. But it was nice to know the man she sat next to could take care of himself in the face of an angry bastard like her ex-husband.

They ended up parking the truck and trailer on Black Water Road, about a mile and a half from the driveway to the Mahon cabin. From there, Bastian and Jenna would ride up into the hills to the ridge indicated on the contour map.

Hopefully, they'd find Earl Monson at the first place they looked. If he'd let them, they'd ask him what he'd seen and glean any information he could tell them, whether it be by hand signals or drawings in the sand, Jenna didn't know. Anyone who might help them locate the McKinnon patriarch was worth the trouble to find.

While Bastian and Parker led the horses out of the trailer, Molly stood with Jenna. "You can clip the walkie talkie to the lapel of your jacket, or if you're afraid you might drop it, you can zip it into your pocket. It'll be harder to get to, but you'll have it in case you get into trouble. Bastian will carry one, too. Hopefully, you two won't get separated. If you do, you'll have the radios to help you reconnect."

"Thank you," Jenna said. "For being here, and for helping us with the walkie talkies."

Molly hugged her. "Just promise me you'll be careful out there. I don't like the idea of you two going without the Montana National Guard. I don't like that there are men in the woods armed with semi-automatic rifles. And I'm all for people owning guns, but not when they're chasing my best friend." Molly hugged her again. "If you see them, get the hell out of there."

"Believe me, I will," Jenna said. "Self-defense classes only go so far to protect you when you're up against an unarmed man, or a man with a knife. All bets off when guns are involved."

"Right." Molly bit her bottom lip. "I feel like we should follow you out there. You know, for backup."

"That's why I have Bastian. Like he said, he has my six." She liked the way that sounded. She knew it was something he did for his teammates. But when he'd told her about it, it had sounded a lot more intimate to her. Or perhaps, it was all wishful thinking that he cared for her more than just because she was Molly's friend.

Bastian cupped his hands and bent low to help Jenna up into the saddle.

She didn't bother to argue with him. She could have reached her foot up into the stirrup and gotten herself up into the saddle. But it was nice of him to help.

Once she was settled, he mounted Little Joe, and Molly handed him a two-way radio.

"Comm check." Parker held up his walkie talkie.

Bastian pressed the button on the side and whispered into the mic. "Test. Test."

Parker nodded and spoke into his mic, "Read you loud and clear." He nodded to Jenna.

She depressed the button on the side and spoke into the mic, "Test. Test."

Molly and Parker both gave a thumbs up.

"Be safe out there and don't be gone past dark," Molly said.

"You sound like Mom," Bastian said with a grin.

"I'll take that as a compliment." Molly smiled. "Now, go."

Jenna nudged Scout in the sides, and the horse broke into a trot.

Bastian carried the small contour map printout and turned his horse into the woods.

Jenna was content to follow his lead. He had training in land navigation through the Navy and BUD/S training. He'd find the cabin, if it was anywhere near that ridgeline.

Jenna shifted in her saddle, her bottom and thighs unused to riding. It had been a long time since she'd been on a horse. She hoped she could last as long as it took to find Mr. Monson.

She'd be damned if she uttered one complaint about the hard saddle. If Bastian could tough it out, so could she.

As they rode off into the woods, Jenna became more concerned about what moved in the shadows rather than her sore bottom.

CHAPTER 7

Bastian led the way into the hills, glancing back often to make sure Jenna was still with him. He preferred to move in on foot where he could control the sounds his movements made, but they had a lot of territory to cover. Especially, if the first cabin wasn't where they would find Earl Monson.

He kept his jacket loose so that he could easily reach the pistol he'd armed himself with in a shoulder holster. The rifle in the scabbard affixed to his saddle was for bigger game.

Not only did they have to be wary of armed two-legged creatures in the woods, they had to be prepared in case they ran across wolves or bears.

He wished he could have completed this mission without Jenna. However, she might be right. If the old man shied away from people, he might not stick around for Bastian to ask questions. Hopefully, he would be more willing to talk to the woman whose life he'd saved.

They found an old trail leading along a creek bank that led upward. With the contour map and a compass in hand, Bastian navigated the terrain, taking detours where the trail was impassible and getting back on track when he could.

Eventually, they came to a wider trail that might once have been an old logging road, now overgrown with brush and saplings. Though it was headed in the direction he wanted to go, he didn't like that it left them exposed to anyone who might be watching.

Hugging the sides of the road in the shadows of mature lodgepole pines, he nudged his horse into a trot, anxious to get to the first cabin. If they had to move on to the second one, they'd need to do so quickly. Already it was past noon, and the sun set thirty minutes to an hour earlier in the mountains than it did on the plains. They would need time to question Monson, and then return to the truck and trailer back on Black Water Road.

He smiled at the thought of Molly and Parker stuck all day at the truck and wondered what they'd do to pass the time. Molly could be impatient, and Parker seemed to be a man who preferred action to standing around twiddling his thumbs.

Parker Bailey was an interesting man with a background much like the McKinnon brothers. He'd been a soldier in the 101st Airborne Division. On his last deployment eight years ago, he'd been injured in a fire-fight. That injury had cost him his career in the military.

He'd returned to Eagle Rock, Montana, his home, around the same time as Marcus Landon, the Iron Horse Ranch foreman, retired and moved to Florida to live with his daughter.

James McKinnon, former military man himself and proud of his sons' choices to serve, heard about Parker and contacted him immediately. At his interview, James hired him on the spot.

Parker had no experience ranching, but he was a decorated war hero and understood the value of hard work and wasn't afraid of long hours. And the animals seemed to like him.

The only person who had any issue with him seemed to be Molly. Twelve years her senior, he ignored her or treated her like a child, which grated on Molly's nerves.

Yeah, it would be a long day for Molly and Parker. If anything, the forced togetherness might help them form a truce.

Ahead, through the trees, Bastian could see a high ridge. The trail wound upward toward it.

The cabin, according to Sheriff Barron's map, would be a few hundred yards below the ridgeline. They should be able to see it soon.

Trees and brush hung low over the trail in some

areas, requiring Bastian and Jenna to duck on many occasions or be brushed off by a limb.

After ducking one such long limb, Bastian emerged on the other side into a small clearing with a log cabin tucked into the far shadowy corner.

He reined his horse to a halt and waited for Jenna to come abreast of him.

"Oh, thank God," she whispered. "I could use a break from this saddle."

Bastian would have laughed, but his tailbone was equally in need of relief.

"How do you want to do this?" she asked.

"I was going to ride across the clearing, dismount and knock on the door," Bastian said.

Jenna frowned. "I think it would be best if I approach alone."

Bastian's fists clenched. "I don't like it."

She raised an eyebrow. "I'd like it even less if Earl snuck out the back door because he didn't want to be bothered with us." Jenna sighed. "Look, I'll go all commando and ease in by sticking close to the tree line and shadows."

"I like that only slightly better." He studied the shadows near the tree line, imagining men in black combat uniforms standing ready to nab her and drag her off to wherever they were hiding his father. "Nope. I don't like it any better."

"Too bad. I'm going." She slipped out of the saddle and staggered a few steps. "After I get my land legs back, that is." When she could stand straight again, she gave him a crooked smile and looped her horse's reins over a low-hanging tree branch. "You've got my six, right?"

He dropped out of his saddle, tied his horse to a tree and pulled the rifle out of the scabbard. "I do now. Go at the door from an angle so I can lock in on whoever comes out of the cabin. It might not be Monson."

Jenna frowned. "Good point. I'll do that."

Bastian leaned against a tree, taking full advantage of the bushes and shadows at its base, and stared down through the sights at the shadowy tree line near the cabin.

Nothing moved. No men in black stood out in the brush. If they were any good, he wouldn't see them. That's what had him worried.

"I really don't like this," he murmured.

"I'm not comfortable with it, either, but someone has to go, and it has to be me." She stepped out of the trees and walked across the clearing, moving quickly, leaving a clear line of fire between him and the cabin door.

Bastian's senses remained on high alert as he scanned the trees, the ridgeline behind the cabin and the structure itself.

As Jenna neared her goal, the door burst open and an old man with a gray, scraggly beard burst out, holding a rifle across his chest.

Bastian aimed at the man and held his fire. "Hello, Earl Monson," he murmured.

If the man brought the rifle up to his shoulder, Bastian would shoot him.

Jenna stopped and held up her hands. "Don't shoot. I came to thank you for saving my life."

The man with the beard jerked his head toward Bastian's position.

Jenna nodded and glanced back at Bastian. "He won't hurt you, as long as you don't hurt me. Earl, I brought him for protection against the men who chased me yesterday."

Monson didn't raise his weapon to his shoulder. He freed one hand and waved at Jenna as if shooing her away.

Jenna shook her head. "I need to talk to you, Mr. Monson."

Even from the distance, Bastian could see the man's eyes widen and then narrow.

"I know who you are," Jenna said. "I'm very sorry about your wife. You must have loved her dearly."

Monson backed into the doorframe and started to close the door.

Jenna took several steps forward. "Please, Mr. Monson, I need to talk to you. We need your help."

He shook his head.

"Please," she said, her voice soft, insistent and compelling.

Had Bastian been Monson, he would have given

Jenna anything she wanted. He held his breath, waiting for Monson to give in and let Jenna talk with him.

Monson paused for a moment, but then shook his head again. The door was closing, along with their chance of getting any information out of him about torture cabin and the victim.

Jenna hurried forward. "Mr. Monson, please. Talk with me."

Suddenly, a flash of fire arched through the air and landed on the wooden shingled roof of the cabin.

Bastian yelled. "Jenna, get down."

She dropped to the ground and lay flat, her hand digging into her jacket for her handgun.

The fire had arrived on the tip of an arrow, fired from somewhere in the shadows of the trees.

Bastian aimed his rifle in that direction.

Another burst of fire launched from the underbrush and landed beside the first arrow, lodged in the wooden shingles.

The fire ignited the wooden shingles and spread across the roof.

Bastian pushed away from the tree and ran toward the position where the arrows had originated.

"Get Monson out of the cabin," he yelled as he passed Jenna and ran into the underbrush.

The sound of an engine revving made Bastian alter direction. He leaped over a fallen log, dodged past a bush and slowed when he saw a man dressed in black, wearing a ski mask, racing away on a four-wheeler.

He didn't go far before he was joined by several other men on a combination of four-wheelers and dirt bikes.

Outnumbered, Bastian turned about and ran back to where Jenna lay on the ground, holding her gun out in front of her.

"Get up. We have to leave. Now!" He bent, grabbed her empty hand and pulled her to her feet. "Run! Get to the horses!"

She pulled free of his hand. "Not without Mr. Monson. They'll kill him."

"Get to the horses," Bastian insisted. "I'll bring Monson."

Jenna was hesitant until she heard the roar of motorcycle engines. Her eyes rounded, and she ran for the horses.

Bastian lunged for the cabin door and slammed his fist against the wooden door. "Monson! Your cabin is on fire, and those men are coming for you. If you want to live, come with us now, or stay and die."

Bastian pounded on the door once more. The engine noises were getting closer. They'd be on them in seconds.

Knowing Jenna wouldn't leave without Monson, Bastian leaned back and was about to kick the door in, when it opened and Monson ran out, coughing and sputtering. Smoke billowed out with him.

Bastian hooked the older man's arm and yelled, "Run!"

Helping Monson as much as he could, he hustled the man across the clearing and shoved him up on Scout. "Can you ride?"

Monson nodded.

"Follow us," Bastian said.

Jenna handed Monson the reins and waited while Bastian swung up into the saddle. He reached down and gripped her forearm and slung her up behind him.

After Jenna wrapped her arms around his waist, Bastian dug his heels into Little Joe's flanks.

The horse leaped forward.

Jenna clung to Bastian as they raced through the woods.

Every so often, Bastian glanced back to make sure Monson was following.

The trip down the mountain went a lot faster than the journey upward, with the dirt bikes and four-wheeler riders hot on their tails.

Bastian pressed the button on the walkie talkie he'd clipped to the lapel of his jacket. "Coming in hot. Could use some backup and firepower," he said.

"Roger. Gotcha covered as soon as you get close enough," Parker fired back.

The good thing about racing downhill through the woods was that their pursuers would be too focused on staying on their rides to manage to shoot with any accuracy. As long as they kept moving and stayed ahead of the others, Bastian, Jenna and Monson would make it to the truck and trailer on Black Water Road.

They had to make it before their pursuers got to a point they could aim and shoot. Monson would be the first one to take a bullet. Then they'd shoot at Bastian and Jenna.

Jenna would take a bullet before Bastian.

He urged his horse to go faster. Jenna was not going to take a bullet. Not today. Not on his watch.

JENNA HELD on tight as the horse plunged down the side of the mountain, over rocky terrain and through the trees. Several times, they turned so fast, she slid sideways and almost fell off. A lunge back in the other direction helped get her back in place.

As the roar of motorcycle engines grew closer, Jenna shot a quick glance over her shoulder. Bless Mr. Monson's heart, the man was right behind them, keeping up as best he could. He bounced and jolted but pressed on.

Beyond Monson and Scout, Jenna could see dirt bikes and four-wheelers dodging around trees and brush, gaining on the horseback riders.

Her breath caught and held until, finally, they burst out onto a gravel road, several yards away from the horse trailer and truck.

Molly stood by the truck and shouted. "Get behind the trailer." She leaned over the hood of the truck with a rifle aimed at the woods.

Jenna didn't wait for the horse to come to a complete stop before she slid off his back and dropped to the ground. She fell to her knees, picked herself up and took up a position beside Molly, with her handgun braced in her palm.

Bastian leaped from the saddle, landed on his feet and pulled out the rifle from the scabbard. He ran around the front of the truck into the woods where he dropped low and aimed his rifle at the oncoming bikes and ATVs.

Monson rode past the truck and trailer and reined his horse to a halt. He slid out of the saddle onto the ground and ducked behind the truck bed.

When the bikers came into range, Bastian and Parker fired.

The lead rider fell from his dirt bike, rolled on the ground and leaped to his feet, holding his side.

The others, apparently seeing the lead rider go down, swerved left or right and circled back.

A four-wheeler driver swept in. The injured rider slipped onto the back of the four-wheeler and the two took off, heading away from the truck and trailer.

The aggressors stopped just out of range of the rifles and faced Bastian, Parker, Molly and Jenna.

Her heart beat so fast, Jenna could barely catch

her breath. Was this what it felt like to be in a stand-off with the enemy in battle? She'd never been so frightened, except when she'd been down, and Corley had kicked her into unconsciousness. Even then, she hadn't been so much frightened as fatalistic. Dying would have been easier.

"What are they waiting for?" Molly asked.

"They're waiting for us to pack it in and leave," Parker said.

"But wouldn't that leave us exposed to them?" Molly asked.

"Yes," Bastian responded. "That's why we're not going anywhere until they leave. Stay behind the truck. If they get by us, roll underneath the truck or trailer."

He didn't have to tell Jenna twice. She was ready. And she would shoot the bastards if they started firing at any one of their party.

The thought of Bastian being hit made her gut clench and sweat pop out on her brow. She prayed all her practice at the gun range would pay off.

Five minutes passed, and the men on bikes didn't come any closer.

Some of them bunched together as if they were in discussion, then they broke apart and faced the truck and trailer again.

She counted six vehicles, plus the one they'd abandoned, made seven riders. Three more people than her, Molly, Bastian and Parker. The bikers outnumbered them, but they didn't have the advantage of cover and concealment.

Another two minutes passed painfully slow. Jenna shifted her weight from one foot to another and kept her gaze on her targets.

"Ever shoot a living being," Molly whispered beside her.

Jenna shivered. "No."

"Never been hunting?" Molly asked.

"No," Jenna said.

"It's different when the target is moving. You have to aim just a little ahead of it."

"Good to know." Every target Jenna had aimed at had been stationary. She prayed she didn't have to shoot a living human, but she would if it was a choice between one of her friends and one of them.

Another minute passed, and the riders turned their bikes and ATVs around and disappeared into the woods.

Parker called out, "Molly & Jenna, we'll cover—"

"And we'll load the horses," Molly finished.

"Monson, get into the truck and lie down on the back floorboard," Bastian called out.

Earl Monson shook his head and started for the opposite side of the road and the woods beyond.

Jenna snagged his arm. "You have to stay with us. We'll make sure you're safe." She led him back to the truck and opened the rear door. "Get in." She spoke firmly and added. "Please. The longer you take, the more likely those jerks will come back."

The older man looked to the woods and back to the truck. Finally, he climbed in and lay down on the floorboard.

Molly had abandoned her position near the truck bed and hurried to round up Little Joe.

Jenna crossed the dirt road to snag Scout's reins and led him up into the back of the trailer. She tied him quickly and exited in time for Molly to load Little Joe. When both horses were in, they closed the gate and latched it.

"Let's go," Molly called out.

Bastian and Parker rose to their feet and stared at the abandoned bike.

"Are you thinking what I'm thinking?" Bastian asked Parker.

Parker nodded. "Let's get that dirt bike."

As the two men tromped through the woods toward the bike, Jenna held her breath and her gun at the ready. They were quickly getting out of range of her ability to provide coverage.

Molly came to stand beside Jenna. "What are they doing?"

"Going after that bike," Jenna said.

"They might be able to identify who the rider is, if they have it," Molly said.

"Yeah, but what if the gang comes back while they're that far out?"

"I have a rifle." Molly said.

"Aren't you afraid you might hit your brother or Parker?" Jenna asked, gauging the distance as around the distance of two football fields. "I wish they'd just leave it and let's get back to the ranch."

"They must think it's importan—" Molly stopped talking as the roar of engines sounded nearby.

The bike and four-wheeler riders roared up the road toward them.

"Damn," Jenna dropped and rolled beneath the truck.

Molly did the same.

Out of the corner of her eye, she could see Bastian and Parker running back toward them, leaping over logs and zigzagging between the trees. They wouldn't get to them in time as far away from the vehicle as they'd gone.

Jenna switched off her safety and aimed at the lead biker and fired a round, doing as Molly suggested and aiming in front of the speeding bike.

A plume of dust kicked up in front of the bike.

Missed.

She raised her aim and fired again.

The bullet hit somewhere on the handlebar. The bike twisted and laid down in the gravel, throwing its rider. A moment later the rider dragged himself off the gravel, his arms and legs scraped raw. He lifted his bike, kickstarted it and rode away.

Molly fired her rifle at the next rider.

The man jerked his hand off the handlebar and slowed.

More shots were fired from the trees where Bastian and Parker had taken cover and were aiming their rifles at the oncoming gang.

The riders kept coming.

Dust rose up around the truck and trailer as the bikers blasted past them.

Molly cursed beside Jenna. "Damned rifle is jammed."

Jenna fired at the wheels rolling past her, unable to focus when the dust and gravel spewed up into her eyes.

The riders spun and raced back at the truck and trailer.

Jenna wouldn't let them get to Mr. Monson. The man was counting on them to protect him.

She rolled on her side and aimed at the rider closest to her and squeezed the trigger.

The man jerked the handlebar of his bike. He didn't fall off, but he didn't slow, either. He drove past the truck and trailer and continued down the road.

The others followed.

When the dust started to settle, Jenna could see that the bikes and four-wheelers were once again waiting out of range of the rifles.

Bastian and Parker appeared beside the truck.

"Get in the truck," Bastian said. "We're leaving."

"What about the bike?" Molly asked.

"It's not worth losing one of you," Parker said. He climbed into the passenger seat and lowered the window, sticking his rifle out.

"Molly, you drive." Bastian opened the back door. "Monson, up on the seat and stay low."

The old man scrambled up onto the seat and bent over.

Jenna climbed in the back on the other side of Earl Monson. "It's going to be all right," she tried to reassure him, though she wasn't even certain that it would be. Like Parker, she lowered her window and positioned herself so that she could use her weapon should she need to.

While Jenna and Bastian had been riding up into the hills, Parker and Molly had turned the truck and trailer around so that they were heading toward Eagle Rock. With the gang of riders behind them, they raced toward town, away from danger and straight to the sheriff's office.

Sheriff Barron listened to their story and sent a couple of his deputies out to investigate. He also alerted the fire department about the cabin on fire in the hills. They would contact the local Hot Shots who would send up a helicopter to evaluate the blaze.

When Sheriff Barron tried to question Earl Monson, the older man curled into his coat and refused to get out of the truck or answer any questions. He sat in stubborn silence.

"What are you going to do with him," the sheriff asked.

"He needs a good meal and a place to sleep," Jenna said. "The poor man has been through a lot today."

"He needs Mom," Molly said.

Bastian frowned. "How do you know he's not dangerous?"

"He saved me from those people," Jenna said.

"He could have been the one who performed the torture," Bastian said, keeping his voice down so that Monson couldn't hear.

Jenna shook her head. "He didn't do those things. He saved me from that same fate. I know it in my gut."

"Are you willing to put the rest of the family at risk by bringing him to Iron Horse Ranch?"

Jenna lifted her chin. "If you think he might be dangerous, you can drop Mr. Monson off at my place in town. I'll stay with him."

Bastian's lips thinned. "You're not going back to your place until we know who those people are and why they were after you, and now, Mr. Monson."

Jenna fisted her hands on her hips. "Then what do you suggest?"

Parker leaned into Bastian. "She has a point."

After a moment of staring into Jenna's eyes, Bastian finally said, "Fine. But we'll take shifts watching him. I don't trust him."

"You don't have to take shifts, I'll keep an eye on

him," Jenna said. "You can put him in my room. I'll sleep outside the door."

"The hell you will." He marched toward the truck, held open the door and jerked his head toward the interior. "Get in."

Jenna cocked an eyebrow and didn't move.

Bastian closed his eyes, drew in a deep breath and opened them again. "Get in, please."

For a moment, Jenna considered telling him to go to hell and to take Mr. Monson to her apartment over the Blue Moose Tavern. Then she thought about all that had happened that day. Mr. Monson wouldn't be safe above the tavern. Those men had lobbed fire-tipped arrows at his cabin. They might do the same to the Blue Moose to burn Earl Monson out.

Monson must know something, or the men in black masked gang wouldn't have followed Jenna and Bastian into the woods, and then burned the cabin down.

What did Monson know, or what had he witnessed that they didn't want to get out?

CHAPTER 8

BASTIAN DROVE with Parker riding shotgun, his rifle at the ready in case they ran into more trouble on the way out to Iron Horse Ranch.

When they arrived, Hank Patterson's big black four-wheel-drive truck was parked in front of the house.

"Good," Bastian said. "Hank's here. Maybe he'll have some news on who might be behind these attacks."

"I'd bet money it's one of the survivalist groups that has been stirring up trouble lately," Parker said.

Bastian's lips pressed into a tight line. "Yeah, but which one and why?" Bastian said.

As he, Parker and Molly climbed out of the truck, Hank, Swede, Angus, Colin and Duncan came out onto the porch. The trio Bastian had come to call the fiancées emerged behind the men: Bree Lansing,

Angus's fiancée; Emily Tremont, Colin's fiancée; and Deputy Fiona Guthrie, Duncan's fiancée who carried their baby Caity on her hip.

An impressive yet somewhat intimidating mob of humanity. Especially for someone who'd been living alone in the backwoods.

Jenna got out of the back seat and leaned into the cab. "Mr. Monson, it's okay. I know you're not used to having all these people around, but they're here to help you. Won't you come inside?"

The old man shook his head.

Bastian could see this was going to be a problem. Monson couldn't sleep all night in the truck. It wasn't an option.

"I'm so glad you all made it back safely. And just in time for dinner." Bastian's mother came out of the house and down the steps, her smile turning into a concerned frown. "What's wrong?"

"Nothing," Bastian said. "But we have another guest we need to find a room for."

"Who have you brought home?" His mother's smile was back in place as she hurried toward the truck and leaned up into the back seat. Her smile faded again as she looked at the man with the long beard and ragged clothing.

Jenna gave her an encouraging smile. "Mrs. McKinnon, this is Mr. Earl Monson."

Bastian's mother's frown disappeared, and her smile returned. "Earl Monson? I thought you'd moved away.

Why yes, I remember you and your dear, sweet wife, Vera." She reached out and touched the man's hand. "I was so sorry to hear about her passing. That was one of the worst winter storms in the history of our state." She squeezed his hand. "Please. Come inside. I made southern fried chicken, mashed potatoes and gravy."

Monson's stomach rumbled even as he shook his head and pulled his hand from beneath Bastian's mother's hand.

"Please, Earl. Vera loved my fried chicken. She would have wanted you to have some." She took his hand again and tugged gently.

At first, the man didn't budge.

Then to Bastian's surprise, Earl Monson let the McKinnon family matriarch draw him out of the truck and up the stairs into the house.

Bastian could hear his mother as she went in. "You can wash your hands in here. I'll wait and show you where the kitchen is."

Jenna came to stand beside Bastian and Molly, shaking her head. "That woman could talk a bear out of hibernation. She's truly gifted."

"That's our mom," Molly said. "She doesn't know a stranger and won't take no for an answer."

"We should let mom feed Mr. Monson first," Molly said. "He might feel more comfortable eating without the usual gang gathered around."

Bastian's mother poked her head out the door.

"You all start supper without us. Earl is going to freshen up before he comes to the table."

Bastian exchanged shocked expressions with Jenna.

"How does she do that?" Jenna asked.

Molly chuckled. "Like you said, it's a gift."

They all moved into the kitchen, determined the table was too small for all of them and moved the food, plates and glasses into the dining room.

"It's a good thing Sadie and Emma are in LA. She'd think I didn't love her cooking as much as I'm over here eating your food," Hank said as he reached for the platter of golden fried chicken. "And don't tell her I had fried chicken. She's got me on a strict, boring diet of vegetables and tofu." Hank shook his head. "What exactly is tofu?" He held up his hand. "No, don't tell me. I'd rather not know. Whatever it is, it's disgusting."

"Then why eat it?" Parker asked.

Hank looked at him with a straight, serious face. "I love my wife. When you love someone as much as I love Sadie, you eat what she fixes and tell her it was the best thing yet."

Angus laughed and turned to Bree. "You wouldn't do that to me, would you?"

Bree gave him a coy look. "What? You didn't like the asparagus I made last night?"

Angus's brow dipped, and his smile disappeared.

"Huh." He leaned over and kissed her cheek. "It's a good thing I love you so much."

Bastian envied Angus and Bree's easy banter and the love apparent in the way they touched and kissed. He was truly happy his brothers had found women they loved with all their hearts.

If he hadn't lost the only woman he'd ever loved in a car accident, he too might be sharing kisses at the table. Eleven years was a long time ago. He could barely remember what Lauren looked like. Only that he'd loved her with all his teenaged heart.

His gaze went to Jenna sitting across the table from him. She smiled and laughed at something Parker said.

Bastian's chest tightened.

Jenna wasn't the same little girl who used to tag along with Molly when they were kids. She was a fully grown and desirable woman. One who deserved a lot better man than Corley Ferguson.

Bastian had played football with Corley. He remembered Corley as someone who didn't always play by the rules. Someone who hit harder than was necessary and, many times, after the play had ended. He'd put a number of opponents and some of his own teammates in the hospital because of how aggressive he played.

The thought of a man who was as big as Corley abusing a woman half his size made Bastian's fists clench and his stomach roil.

Jenna deserved to find someone who would treat her like a woman should be treated. She'd always been kind to him. Even when he'd been short with her. She was gentle with her mountain man, when Bastian wanted to get straight down to the business of finding out what the old man knew.

Although anxious to know what Monson might have seen, Bastian was forced to wait.

After everyone had food on their plates, Hank dove in. "The sheriff called and let us know what happened when you went in search of Mr. Monson. That's part of the reason we came. We're glad you made it out safely."

"Thanks," Bastian said. He glanced around at the others at the table. "I guess you all know what happened then?"

Everyone nodded.

"And Mom?" he asked.

"She knows," Angus said.

"Good." At least he didn't have to rehash their adventure.

"Swede and I did some footwork and cyber snooping to find out more about the preppers and survivalist organizations in the area near Eagle Rock."

Jenna glanced sharply at Hank. "Who are they?"

"Some of them have been around for a while. Others are new startups, fed up with government controls and legislation," Hank said.

"One of the survivalist factions, in particular, has an online social media group they post to," Swede said. "They call themselves the Snake Dragons."

Jenna's face paled. "They're the ones who attacked me first."

"How do you know it was them?" Bastian asked.

She met Bastian's gaze. "One of the men who chased me from the torture cabin had a tattoo on his forearm. It appeared to be a snake on one end and a dragon on the other."

"They're very active, and secretive," Swede said. "All their messages are in code. I have yet to decipher them."

"I have access to an FBI agent with excellent drone skills," Hank said. "She's willing to fly her drone over the nearby foothills to see if we can locate the survivalists' camp."

"That would be great," Angus said. "How soon can we get her out here?"

Hank grinned. "Oh, she's local. She's engaged to Kujo, one of my former Delta Force guys. He'll come out with her and bring his military war dog, Six." Hank glanced at Molly. "You and the FBI agent have something in common," he said.

Molly frowned. "Does she have four pushy brothers?"

Hank laughed. "No, but she has your name, Molly. Molly Greenbriar. I think you'll like her."

Molly grinned. "How could I not?"

Hank's lips twisted. "True. Ms. Greenbriar could be out here as soon as tomorrow morning."

"The sooner the better," Bastian said. "If the survivalists are involved in my father's disappearance, we need to find them and bring my father home."

His brothers nodded agreement.

"You think the survivalists are after the money?" Colin asked.

"I think everyone is after that money,"

Jenna's head dipped. "Actually, even the insurance company for the bank is looking."

Bastian frowned. "How do you know?"

She lifted her head and stared straight into his eyes. "They pay me to keep an eye out for possible locations the money could be hidden."

"Why didn't you tell us that?" Bastian asked.

She shrugged. "Compared to what I saw in that cabin, I didn't think it was important. It slipped my mind until now."

Hank and Swede exchanged glances.

Hank faced Jenna. "Let us have the name of the insurance company and your contact. We'll do some digging into his background and the insurance company's track record."

Jenna's brow twisted. "You think the insurance company had something to do with the torture and attacks?"

"We have to check out all possible suspects," Hank

said. "Sometimes, the least likely suspect ends up being the one who did it." Hank gave her his cellphone number.

"Forwarding the contact name and phone number I have on my cellphone, now." She glanced down at her cellphone, scrolled through her contacts, selected send, entered Hank's number and hit send. A moment later, she grimaced. "No service."

"Sorry. Cellphone reception is almost nonexistent out here," Molly said. "Tap into our WIFI." Molly gave her the password, and Jenna was able to join the network.

Meanwhile, Hank clicked the screen on his cellphone and entered the WIFI network.

Once Jenna was in, she found the name and number for her contact and forwarded the information to Hank.

"Got it," Hank said. "I'll get Ms. Greenbriar out here tomorrow. You can show her the area where the attacks have taken place. It's likely their camp isn't far from there."

"We'll be ready," Bastian said.

Hank carried his plate to the sink and glanced out the window. "Looks like we'll have a clear sky. I need to get back to the White Oak Ranch and take care of my animals. If you need me, you know how to reach me."

Swede rose, grabbing a dinner roll from the basket in the middle of the table. "I guess I'm leaving too, since Hank's my ride. Tell Mrs. McKinnon thanks. The chicken was perfect."

"Yes. Please thank your mother for dinner and remind her not to tell Sadie I had anything fried." He winked and left the kitchen.

Moments later the front door closed with a click.

"Did Hank leave?" Bastian's mother asked as she entered the kitchen.

"Yes, ma'am," Parker said.

"He and Swede said to tell you thanks for the fried chicken. It's the best they've ever had," Molly said.

"Oh, it's a shame they didn't stay long enough to meet the Earl Monson I knew and loved." She turned in the doorway and glanced behind her. "It's okay. They're just finishing up supper. Come on in."

A man Bastian barely recognized stepped through the door, cleanshaven, his shaggy hair slicked back from his forehead, and wearing clean jeans and a plaid flannel shirt. The shirt and jeans were too big, but they were a far cry better than the smelly clothing he'd worn earlier.

"Ladies and gentlemen," his mother said. "This is Earl Monson, a dear friend."

Earl nodded, looking up briefly at the faces in the room before he lowered his head and started to turn.

He's going to make a run for it, Bastian guessed.

His mother hooked Earl's arm, preventing him from darting away. "Since everyone else is finished with supper, won't you stay and keep me company while I eat?"

Earl looked from the faces at the table to Bastian's mother and back.

Jenna pushed her chair back. "I think it would be a good idea to move this conversation to the living room and give Mrs. McKinnon and Mr. Monson a chance to eat their dinner."

Everyone seemed to move at once, carrying their dishes to the counter beside the sink.

"I'll do the dishes when your mother is finished eating," Jenna promised.

"And I'll help," Molly added. "It is a beautiful night. Why don't we adjourn to the front porch and enjoy the stars that only shine this brightly in Montana?"

Everyone but Bastian's mother and Earl Monson left the kitchen.

Bastian paused at the door. All cleaned up, Earl didn't look like the crazed mountain man who'd saved Jenna's life. Still, he was the same man, and Bastian was on the fence over leaving his mother with Earl.

His mother guided Earl to the table and urged him to take a seat. "Smells good, doesn't it?" she said with a smile. When she noticed Bastian at the door, her brow dipped briefly. "You don't have to stay, Bastian. Earl and I are going to catch up on old times. His wife, Vera, and I used to be in the same quilting club." She patted the man's arm. "We have a lot to talk about, don't we?"

Earl didn't answer, but he reached up and covered her hand with his. And were those tears in the old man's eyes?

Bastian nodded. "If you need anything, all you have to do is yell. We'll be on the front porch with the door open to let fresh air in." *And noises out.*

Hopefully, Monson would get the message that they'd be listening for trouble.

His mother nodded and waved a hand at him, shooing him out of the kitchen. "Go on. We're hungry, and you're holding us up from digging into what's left of the fried chicken."

Reluctantly, Bastian left the kitchen and walked down the hallway and out onto the front porch.

Duncan sat with Fiona on the porch swing, holding Caity in his lap. Angus and Bree sat side by side in matching rocking chairs, holding hands and staring out into the darkness lit up by a billion twinkling stars. Colin stood with an arm around Emily's shoulders, stargazing as well.

Molly sat on the steps, her back leaning against the post, her eyes closed.

Parker stood in the yard, his hands in his pockets. His gaze wasn't on the heavens but on the pasture. The man worked all the time. He was probably thinking about what needed to be done the next day.

Only one person was missing from the scene.

"Where's Jenna?" Bastian asked.

"I don't know," Angus replied. "She was here a moment ago."

"She went out to the barn," Parker said.

"By herself?"

"I asked her if she wanted company." Parker shrugged. "She said she preferred to be alone."

His senses on alert, Bastian stepped down from the porch and hurried out to the barn. Jenna had been attacked on more than one occasion in the past forty-eight hours. The Iron Horse Ranch wasn't on lockdown, nor did they have guards on the gates, the house or barn to keep trespassers from walking in, fully loaded and ready to rumble.

Bastian opened the barn door. The lights were on, casting a soft yellow glow throughout. A horse pawed the ground as if it was irritated by the disturbance.

"Jenna?" Bastian called out.

Nothing.

"Jenna?" he called out more forcefully.

She popped out of the tack room, a frown denting her brow. "I thought I heard someone. Hi, Bastian. Can I help you with something?"

"You can help by getting back to the house," he said, his voice a little more cross than he wanted it to be. But, dammit, she'd worried him.

She propped her fists on her hips. "Look, I appreciate your help in keeping me alive, but I have to keep moving or I'll go nuts." She sighed. "I should be working. Every day I'm out of the office, it takes twice as long to get back into the swing. I need to go back to work."

"You can't," he said, firmly. "Not while you're at risk of being shot, kidnapped or killed."

She shook her head. "You don't understand. If I don't work, I don't earn. If I don't earn, I can't pay my bills or save for a house of my own."

"I understand. Yet if you go out showing property, you might be attacked again. You don't need to earn money or pay rent if you're dead."

Her shoulders sagged. "You're right, and you know how I am about winning an argument."

"Fanatical?" He smiled down at her. "I remember." He reached out and captured her arms in his hands. "You would run harder and faster than any guy in school, just to prove a point."

"And yet, you're in the Navy SEALs, saving the world, while I'm rotting away in a small town, working for peanuts and scarce paychecks that don't come often enough." Jenna sighed. "You've seen and done it all."

"Not all," he said.

"What haven't you done that you regret not doing?" she whispered.

His mind skimmed over the images of his brothers holding onto their women. He'd never seen them happier, and he found himself envious of their newfound joy.

Was he wrong to deny himself that same joy? Would Lauren have wanted him to grieve for her for the rest of his life?

He stared down at Jenna, his promise to Lauren having faded with time and the realization he couldn't grieve forever.

"I haven't kissed you," he said, his gaze dropping to her full, luscious lips.

Her eyes rounded, and a deeply indrawn breath made her chest rise and brush against his. "Life is short," she said. "No regrets." She slid her hand up his chest, circled the back of his neck and brought his mouth down to hers.

Sweet Jesus, what were they doing?

Bastian couldn't help it. He had to kiss her. Had to hold her in his arms. Gathering her closer, he crushed her in his arms and bent to take what she offered, and then some.

What began as a light brush of her lips across his, quickly morphed into an intensity of emotion that robbed him of his senses.

CHAPTER 9

JENNA CLUNG TO BASTIAN, her arms wrapped around his neck, her hips pressed hard against his. She could feel the rise of his desire, nudging her belly, and she wanted so much more.

All her teenaged angst was nothing compared to the tidal wave of longing...no...lust rising up to consume her. She'd never felt like this with Corley. She hadn't known these kinds of feelings existed. She'd never considered that the kind of desire she'd found in fiction was real.

Boy howdy, it was.

She opened to him, meeting his tongue with hers, countering every one of his thrusts, tangling, toying and teasing until she gasped for breath.

Still, it wasn't enough.

Jenna moved her hands down to his chest and

worked the buttons free on his shirt, one at a time, frustrated by how long it was taking.

Bastian grabbed the hem of her cotton sweater and yanked it over her head. Then he must have remembered where they were. He scooped her into his arms and carried her up the wooden staircase to the loft above.

She loved how strong he was. He didn't even breathe hard as he climbed the stairs.

Once in the loft with the pungent scent of hay surrounding them, he lowered her feet to the ground and kissed her again.

He started slowly, exploring her mouth then her cheek, the sensitive spot below her earlobe and down the column of her neck to linger where her pulse beat frantically.

"Bastian," she breathed. "You're killing me."

"Sweetheart, it's a two-way street."

"Then let me get this race car rolling," she said and reached for the button on his jeans, flicking it open. Then she lowered the zipper ever so slowly, careful not to hurt him.

His shaft sprang free, making her smile. The man was a Navy SEAL. Of course, he went commando.

She palmed his staff, weighing it in her hand, testing the hardness, the girth and the length. Holy hell, he was big. And she wanted him.

Inside. Now.

Jenna let go of him, reached behind her back and

unclipped her bra, letting the straps slide down her arms.

"Are you sure you want this?" he asked.

She looked up at him in the dim light from the bulb burning in another part of the barn. "Never more certain of anything in my life."

When she slid her hands into the waistband of his jeans, he gripped her arms and stopped her. "I want you to know, I would never intentionally hurt you," he said. "I'm not that kind of man."

She looked up into his eyes. "I know. I wouldn't be with you, if you were."

Still, he wouldn't release her arms to let her continue stripping him.

"If at any time you change your mind about what we're doing, all you have to do is tell me," he said. "I'll stop."

Again, she stared into his eyes. "I know."

Then he smiled, that incredibly sexy smile that melted her knees and other wetter places in her body. Jenna almost swooned but held it together for what would come next.

She worked his jeans down over his buttocks, while kicking off her boots.

He toed off his boots and worked on the button on her jeans, fumbling to the point she shoved his hands aside and released the button herself. She unzipped and shimmied out of the denim, letting it pool at her ankles in the loose hay.

"Have you ever lain naked in the hay?" he asked.

She shook her head. "No. Have you?"

He nodded. "It's not as sexy as it sounds. We could dress and go back inside and up to our rooms."

Jenna shook her head. "Not an option. I'll take my chances." She stepped out of her jeans and stood in nothing but a pair of silky pink panties.

Bastian stepped free of his jeans and stood naked, his cock jutting outward, straight, thick and hard.

He pulled her into his arms, tilted her head upward and claimed her lips in a hungry kiss that rocked her soul and made her long for more. She wrapped her arms around his neck and pressed her breasts to his chest, loving the way the coarse hairs tickled her skin and teased her nipples.

Bastian bent and clutched the backs of her thighs and lifted her, wrapping her legs around his waist. His cock touched her weeping entrance, the tip teasing the entrance. "Damn," he muttered.

"What? Did I do it wrong?" she asked.

"No, no. You're doing everything right. It's me." He dropped her feet back to the ground and lunged for his jeans, pulling his wallet from the back pocket. "I hope I have one…" He flipped open the black leather billfold and riffled through the contents until he exclaimed, "Thank God." He held up a square packet.

Jenna took it from him and would have applied it

to his erection right then. She was hot and wet. She didn't know if she could wait much longer.

"Not yet," he said and covered her hand with his. "Hold onto that. It's the only one I have here."

"But I'm ready. Now."

He shook his head. "Not yet." Bastian kissed her lips, her cheek, her neck and lower. He bent to take one of her breasts into his mouth, tonguing, nipping and flicking the nipple until it beaded into a tight little knot.

"Now?" she moaned, her core heating to an inferno, her fingers sliding over his shoulders, digging into his skin.

"Not yet."

She was beginning to hate those two words. If he didn't come into her soon, she'd take matters into her own hands and make it happen.

That's when Bastian dropped to his knees on the hay and nudged apart her thighs.

Jenna's breath caught and lodged in her lungs as his hand cupped her sex, massaging the puff of hair there. Then he parted her folds and slipped a finger into her channel.

She moaned and rocked her hips. Her fingers wove through his hair, kneading his scalp. What was he doing to her? She didn't feel like she had any control whatsoever over her body or its response to what he was doing. And for someone who liked having control, she suddenly didn't care. He could do anything he wanted with her, as long as he continued to do what he was doing along with it.

He drew his wet finger up between her folds and teased her clit, swirling, flicking and strumming that little bit of nerve-packed flesh, until Jenna whimpered and her knees wobbled.

When he replaced his finger with his tongue, it was all she could do not to scream aloud. "Bastian," she whispered. "Oh, dear, sweet Bastian. I'm going to..." Her breath hitched, and her body quaked with a release so intense, Jenna thought she'd died and gone to heaven.

He played her with his tongue until she could barely remain upright. She pulled at his hair. "Please," she begged. "I want you."

Bastian flicked her once more with his tongue and then rose to his feet, captured her mouth with his and kissed her.

She could taste herself on his tongue, and it made her even more anxious to have him fill her to full, to take up all the empty space her ex-husband had hammered into her.

When he stepped back, she tore open the packet she'd held in her hand all this time and rolled the contents over his shaft, reveling in the velvety smooth strength beneath her fingertips.

Then he was lifting her, wrapping her legs around his waist and lowering her until his cock pressed into her channel.

"I'll take it slow. I don't want to hurt you," he said.

"Oh, please," she said and lowered herself over him in one smooth, descent, taking all of him down to the base of his shaft.

He filled her, his girth stretching her tight. When he moved, she arched and threw her head back. This was what she'd wanted. To ride this cowboy. "Make it hard and fast," she whispered.

He backed her up to a post and leaned her back against the smooth wood. Then, holding her hips in his grip, he slammed into her, again and again, moving faster with each thrust.

Her hands on his shoulders, Jenna rode the McKinnon all the way until he thrust his last, sinking deep inside her. His hands on her buttocks held her firmly, while his shaft throbbed and pulsed against her slick channel.

Bastian buried his face against her throat, pressing his lips against her skin.

For a long moment, he held her tight until, finally, he let go of the breath he'd been holding and relaxed. "Are you okay?" he asked as he loosened his grip on her ass.

She nodded, a tentative smile, curling her lips. "Are you?"

Bastian laughed, slid out of her and lowered her to her feet. "Never better." He retrieved the condom packaging, removed the protection from his still-hard erection and tucked it into the package. With his free hand, he cupped the back of her head and tipped her chin up. "You're amazing."

"You're not so bad, yourself," she said, suddenly shy standing there naked in front of him in the middle of the loft full of hay bales.

Then he kissed her lips gently, stripping away any shyness and leaving her ready for round two.

The sound of a door creaking open captured her attention. Her gaze flew to his, and her eyes widened.

Bastian pressed a finger to his lips.

"Bastian, Jenna?" Molly's voice sounded from below.

Jenna shook her head and pressed a finger to her lips, just like he had.

He captured her and kissed the tip of her finger before calling out. "We're in the loft."

"Everything okay?" Molly asked. "Do you need help?" Her voice seemed to be moving closer.

Jenna's heart beat faster, and she scrambled, searching for her jeans and shirt, remembering a moment later that her shirt was somewhere below where they'd begun their little strip show.

"We don't need help," Bastian responded.

"Are you sure?" she persisted.

Jenna found her jeans, frantically shoved her feet into the legs and dragged them up over her hips.

Bastian stood there, not at all concerned about being naked or getting dressed. "Everything is under control up here. No need to stick around. I'm sure you have better things to do."

"Jenna?" Molly called out.

"I'm fine," Jenna squeaked. She cleared her throat and forced her voice to calm. "We'll be back at the house in a few minutes. I was looking for the stray cat that used to live up here."

"That cat's been gone for years," Molly said.

"Oh. Well, then, we won't be much longer," Jenna said.

"Okay. I'll see you at the house," Molly said.

Jenna let go of the breath she'd been holding and waited for the sound of the door creaking open and closed. It creaked open, but then there was a pause.

"If you're looking for your bra and shirt, I laid them over the first stall door," Molly called out.

Jenna clapped a hand over her mouth, mortified that her friend had seen her clothing.

The door hinge creaked, and the click of the door closing was the only sound in the now silent barn.

Bastian threw back his head and laughed so hard, he bent over, clutching at his naked sides.

"It's not funny," Jenna said. Despite her mortification, her lips twitched, and a chuckle rose up her throat, erupting into a full belly laugh that brought tears to her eyes. "How...am I ...going to explain... this?" she said through the ensuing hiccups.

"You're not. It's none of Molly's business." Bastian leaned over and kissed the tip of her nipple. "Do you want me to retrieve your bra and shirt and bring them up here?"

"Yes," she said. "After you put on your jeans. No telling who else will wander out here looking for us."

Bastian pulled on his jeans and boots and ran down the stairs. He was back in seconds with her bra and shirt.

When she reached out, he held them back. "Whatcha gonna give me in exchange for one bra and one shirt?"

She held up her fist. "A knuckle sandwich." When he didn't give in, she frowned. "Fine." She stood up on her toes and pressed her lips to his. "Now, will you give me my clothes?"

"Mmm." He shook his head. "I like you like this."

"Give me my clothes," she said and attacked him, throwing her arms around his waist, trying to reach for the items he held behind his back.

"See? There was a method to my madness." His arms switched directions, and he wrapped them around her, pulling her close. "That little peck wasn't nearly sincere enough." He proceeded to show her the difference.

Minutes later, after being thoroughly kissed, Jenna fumbled with her bra, her hands shaking and her knees feeling like jelly.

Bastian helped her slip her shirt over her head and pulled it down her torso, his knuckles grazing the skin of her breasts.

"When did you say we'd be back at the house?" she whispered.

"I didn't. You did. And the answer is soon. Much too soon." He bent to kiss the base of her throat and tongued the pulse thundering there.

"If we hurry..." Jenna grabbed the hem of her shirt, ready to pull it over her head.

He covered her hand with his. "I don't have another condom."

She let the air out of lungs like a deflating balloon. "Oh, that's too bad."

He kissed the tip of her nose. "Agreed."

"I guess there's nothing left to do but head back to the house."

Bastian tucked the hem of his shirt into the waistband of his jeans. "You have some hay in your hair." He plucked a straw from her hair and trailed it down the V-neck of her sweater. "Ready?"

She sucked in a breath as the straw slipped over the swell of her breast. "Yes," she half-whispered and half-hissed.

"Good." He took her hand and led her toward the door. "I think Mom made apple pie, and there's a gallon of vanilla ice cream in the freezer."

"Food?" Jenna shook her head. "You can think of food?"

"Sure. I worked up an appetite." He grinned and held open the door for her.

Jenna shook her head as she passed through.

A sharp slap to her bottom made her jump. She spun, rubbing her backside. "You didn't."

"Oh, yes, I did." Then he winked. "And I'd do it again, given half a chance. Now, about that ice cream." He marched past her.

Jenna swung her arm, aiming for his glorious ass.

Before her hand connected, he grabbed her wrist and held it. "Gotta be quicker than that."

"Jerk."

"That's one of the nicer things I've been called." He kept hold of her hand and walked back to the house.

Molly stood at the top of the stairs, leaning against a post, grinning like a fool. "Find that cat you were looking for?" she asked.

Colin frowned. "What cat?"

"Oh, did I say cat?" Molly covered her mouth playfully. "I meant pus—"

Jenna grabbed Molly's arm and yanked her toward the house. "Isn't there something we need to wash—" leaning closer to Molly's ear, she finished her question in a whisper, "like your mouth out with soap?"

Molly giggled. "I'm not the one who was chasing kitties in the barn."

"What kitties?" Colin asked. "I thought they were gone."

"Ask Jenna," Molly called out as Jenna dragged her through the door and into the house.

Molly hugged her arm. "So, tell me all about it."

"No way."

"Why not? I know you've had a thing for Bastian since forever."

"I don't want to talk about it," Jenna said.

"I'm your best buddy. We share everything."

Jenna shook her head. "Not this. Not yet."

Perhaps the tone of her voice finally got to Molly, because she didn't push. "Well, if it means anything to you, I'm glad for you two. It's about time things went right for you two in the love department."

Jenna, her eyes filling with tears, hugged her friend, and then ran up the stairs to her room.

It was too soon to talk about what had happened in the barn. She didn't know what it meant, or if it would ever happen again. Bastian hadn't said anything about what came next. For all she knew, it was a once in a lifetime event, and he'd forget about her as soon as he returned to active duty.

She entered her room, closed the door, leaned her back against it and slid to the floor.

God, she hoped it meant more than that to him, because making love to Bastian meant everything to her.

CHAPTER 10

BASTIAN WANTED to join Jenna in her room that night. But every time he left his room to go to hers, someone was in the hall.

First, it was Molly, sneaking down the stairs for a snack. Then, it was Fiona, slipping down to the kitchen for a bottle for Caity. By the time the coast was clear, it was well past eleven.

He knocked gently on the door. If she was awake, she'd answer. If not, well…he'd go back to his room and try to sleep.

She hadn't responded to his knock, and he went back to his room to stare up at the ceiling until the early hours of the morning when he finally drifted off.

During those long hours of sleeplessness, he questioned everything about his relationship with Jenna.

From the fact she was Molly's friend to his commitment to the US Navy. Finally, he'd wrestled with his vow to Lauren, that he would never love another woman.

The problem was, he was falling in love with Jenna. If anything happened to her...

He couldn't go through that again.

Bastian had suffered through the most grueling training on the planet when he'd gone through BUD/S training to become a SEAL. Still, it hadn't been nearly as hard as losing Lauren with the second-guessing and guilt he'd harbored for years.

SEAL training was cut and dried. More physical than mental. He could handle physical pain. Emotional suffering took too big a toll.

Falling in love with Jenna could only lead to heartbreak.

As he drifted into sleep, he relived in his dreams making love to her in the hay loft. His kid sister's friend was a passionate woman he could happily make love to for the rest of his life.

He woke with the dawn and a headache from too little sleep and too many thoughts spinning around his consciousness. What he needed was to get outside, breathe and get his head on straight.

Finding his father was the number one reason for taking leave. Not making love to a beautiful real estate agent.

He dressed and crossed to the bathroom to brush his teeth, shave and run a comb through his hair. When he left the bathroom, his gaze went to Jenna's room.

The urge to knock on her door was almost overwhelming. Dear Lord, he was obsessing over a female.

Bastian squared his shoulders and marched down the stairs to the kitchen.

Half the family was already up, making coffee and breakfast. His mother manned the spatula in front of the stove. Angus hovered around the coffee maker, waiting for it to stop dripping. Colin was putting the dishes away from the dishwasher.

And standing at the toaster was the woman who'd occupied every one of Bastian's thoughts throughout the night.

Jenna turned as he entered the kitchen, a soft flush of color filling her cheeks. "Do you want toast with your eggs?" she asked.

He nodded.

The color deepened in her cheeks. Was she feeling as awkward as he was? "One slice or two?"

"Two," he answered. He didn't want toast at all. He wanted to swing her up into his arms, carry her up to his room and make sweet love to her in a real bed, not a hay loft. He wanted to wake in the morning with her in his arms and do it all over again.

Sweet Jesus, he had it bad. "I'm going to check on the animals. I'll be back in a minute."

"Duncan and Parker are out there now," his mother said.

"I'll see if they need help." Bastian was halfway across the kitchen when Duncan and Parker came through the back door, talking about one of the horses.

"Need any help with the animals?" Bastian asked.

Duncan's brow twisted. "All taken care of, for now."

At a loss for what to do with himself, Bastian stepped out on the porch anyway. He stared at the blue Montana sky. He thought it ironic how nature managed to go on unimpeded by the goings on of the human race. The sun rose every day and set every day, whether Bastian got a good night's sleep or not.

"Breakfast is ready," his mother called out.

Bastian drew in a deep breath of pure Montana air and entered the kitchen.

Jenna had taken a seat at the table. Angus had taken the seat on one side of her. Bree sat at his other side.

The seat on Jenna's other side was empty.

Bastian started for the seat, but Colin beat him to it. Emily sat on the other side of him. Which left the chair between his mother and Mr. Monson. Bastian settled there, trying to look in Jenna's direction, as his gaze was wont to do, automatically.

As soon as the family settled at the table, a knock sounded on the front door.

"I'll get it." Bastian's mother popped up from her seat as if she had a spring built into her backside. She hurried out of the room.

The sound of a male voice and a female voice came from down the hallway. His mother said something, and footsteps tapped on the wood flooring.

His mother appeared in the doorway with a woman, a man and a German Shepherd.

"This is Special Agent Molly Greenbriar and Joseph Kuntz, but he says you can call him Kujo. And since we have a Molly McKinnon, you can call Kujo's Molly, by her last name, Greenbriar, to keep from getting confused." She leaned forward and pointed to the dog. "The hairy one is retired military war dog, Six." Bastian's mother beamed. "I offered them food, but they insisted they've already had their breakfast."

Kujo waved a hand. "Don't let us stop you. We'll wait outside on the porch until you're done."

Kujo and Special Agent Greenbriar turned and walked back the way they'd come. Six looked around at the people at the table, then turned and followed the couple out of the house.

Bastian finished his eggs and toast and carried his plate to the sink.

Jenna stepped up beside him and murmured, "Good morning," as she laid her plate and fork in the sink on top of his. She lifted her chin and met his gaze with a twisted brow. "Did you sleep all right?"

He nodded, while every nerve in his body screamed for him to take her in his arms and give her a proper good-morning kiss. Somehow, he managed to contain himself. "Did you sleep well?"

Her gaze dropped from his. "I did." For a moment, she stood in front of him.

God, Bastian wanted to take her into his arms and crush her body against his.

The moment passed, and Jenna turned and walked away.

What the hell was he doing? Was he punishing himself for the desire raging through his body?

Bastian followed Jenna out onto the porch where Greenbriar and Kujo waited.

"Hi, I'm Jenna. Bastian and I are going with you today," Jenna said before Bastian could say anything different.

"I think the earlier the better," Greenbriar said. "Hopefully, they won't expect a drone to fly over their heads."

"Is it very loud?" Jenna asked.

"Not very," Ms. Greenbriar said. "But if they have anything going on in the camp, hopefully, they won't notice."

"How soon do you want to leave?" Bastian asked, ready to get out there, find the camp and stage a raid to find his father.

"We're ready when you are," Kujo said.

Bastian nodded. "Give us a few minutes to load the four-wheelers."

Duncan stepped out on the deck. "Angus and Colin are going with you, too."

"Good," Bastian said. "We're not trying to get close to them on the four-wheelers. We only want to get the drone close enough to locate them. Once we know where they are, we can go in on foot and see if they really are holding Dad hostage."

"That's the plan," Kujo said. "And Hank's got his guys on call, including me. We can be ready to go in less than a couple of hours."

Bastian backed his truck up to the utility trailer while Jenna, Angus, Colin and Duncan brought the four-wheelers out of the barn. They loaded the four ATVs onto the trailer.

He cornered Jenna before she got into the truck. "I would rather you didn't go."

"Like you said, we aren't getting close enough for them to hear us. We should be safe. Besides, I feel like I have some skin in this game. They've attacked me twice. I'm taking it personally. I want to know where the hell they are, too."

"When we go into that camp, you're not coming with us," he said, his tone firm.

Jenna's eyes narrowed.

"You're not combat trained. You could slow or compromise the mission."

She drew in a breath and let it out slowly. "I'll give you that. But you have to promise you'll give them hell for me."

He held up his hand as if swearing in court. "I promise." His lips quirked on the corners.

"Okay, then." She leaned up on her toes and pressed a kiss to his lips. "I don't know what I did to make you mad, but I still like you." She winked and ducked into the back seat of the truck.

Bastian's lips tingled where she'd kissed him. He'd tried to keep his distance from her, but he could see it was going to be a challenge. It didn't help that she was sexy and sassy. He admired that in a woman. She was strong and determined. It was then he realized that Jenna and Lauren were as different as two women could be. Lauren had been shy and content to let him make the decisions. She liked that he took care of her and made her feel protected.

Not Jenna. She'd gone through hell with her first husband and made it clear she could take care of herself.

Though Bastian and Lauren had made love, theirs was young, inexperienced sex. Lauren had been embarrassed to be naked in front of him.

Not Jenna. She'd been as excited and eager to get naked as Bastian had been, and she hadn't cared that it was in a barn in a hay loft.

Angus claimed the driver's seat, and Colin called

shotgun. Which left Bastian the back seat next to Jenna.

They'd loaded the truck with rifles and handguns for each of them. Jenna had her handgun strapped to her beneath her jacket.

Kujo and Greenbriar followed them in the truck they'd brought with two four-wheelers loaded on the trailer they pulled.

"I don't think it's a great idea to go to the same spot on Black Water Road as we did yesterday," Bastian said. "We want to get close to that area, but they'll be expecting us to be there. I say we park the trucks out of sight on the main highway and take the ATVs in, but not too close."

Angus nodded. "Makes sense." He drove the rest of the way in silence. As they neared Black Water Road, they searched for a place where they could park both trailers out of sight. Finally, Bastian noticed a road leading off the main highway. They turned off onto the gravel road and found themselves in a large gravel pit, where they were able to turn the trucks and trailers around to face the road out.

Once they'd parked, they unloaded the four-wheelers and lined them up.

Greenbriar got the drone out of the backseat of their pickup and strapped it to the rack on the front of her four-wheeler. She tucked the remote control in her jacket pocket.

Kujo unfolded a map on the hood of his truck and

oriented himself. He pointed at a position on the map. "We're here," he said.

Bastian leaned closer and studied the map. It was a contour map depicting the elevations, hill tops and some of the roads leading into the mountains. "The cabin they used to torture their victim is here." He pointed at the road that led from Black Water Road to the cabin where Jenna had seen the blood, chair and battery. Then he pointed to the ridgeline beneath which was the hunter's cabin their attackers had burned the day before. "We were here yesterday. I'd say the camp has to be really close to this area." He drew a circle with his finger.

Kujo took over, pointing at the map. "We can take this gravel road as far as it goes. Once we find a decent clearing, Molly can launch the drone and do her thing."

Once they were all in agreement, they strapped on their helmets and drove down the side of the highway until they found the gravel road leading into the forest.

Kujo took the lead, followed by Greenbriar, Angus, Bastian and Jenna. Colin brought up the rear. Six ran alongside Kujo, keeping up easily as the four-wheelers had to move around fallen trees and ditches.

For several miles, they wound through the trees on what once might have been a logging or old mining road. The road was narrow, and in many places, not much more than a trail.

At one point, Kujo stopped, pulled out the map and reoriented. Six laid down at his side, panting.

Bastian was surprised they hadn't gotten any farther than they had, but then, they were in the woods and traveling on an overgrown road.

After a few minutes, they mounted up and continued climbing. When they came to the top of a hill, the trees opened up into a small clearing, exposed to the sunshine and blue skies.

Kujo stopped his ATV on the edge of the clearing. The others followed suit, leaving the center of the clearing free for Molly to launch her drone.

As soon as she had the drone on the ground, Greenbriar pulled the remote control out of her pocket and switched it on. Moments later, she had the drone hovering off the ground, rising into the air. She stared at a small video screen displaying what the drone could see from its vantage point in the sky.

Angus, Colin, Jenna and Bastian gathered around Greenbriar as she maneuvered the drone up over the trees and escarpments, slowly flying it over the hills and valleys to the southwest.

"See anything?" Kujo asked as he bent to scratch behind Six's ear.

Greenbriar shook her head. "Nothing yet. But then, the screen is really small. The good thing is that it's sending signals back to Swede with the GPS coordinates of positions where the camera is pointing. Back at the White Oak Ranch, Swede can go over the footage and enlarge the images. They'll be able to see more than we can."

She worked the drone for the next thirty minutes, maneuvering it back and forth over the terrain.

"Gotta bring it in," Greenbriar said. "The battery is getting low." She shifted the controls, bringing the drone back in their direction.

"How far out is it?" Jenna asked.

"About three kilometers, getting closer," the FBI agent said. "We should be able to see it when it's within about a thousand feet of our location." For the next few minutes, they watched the images the drone was creating.

"Look for it," Greenbriar said, her gaze turning from the screen in front of her to the sky.

Bastian looked, but couldn't see the drone, even though he could hear the buzz of the little engine.

She pointed. "There. Over the top of the really tall pine."

Bastian looked again. This time, he saw the drone moving toward them. At that moment, the sound of motorcycle engines roared in the distance, and an awful thought occurred to him. If they could see the drone, couldn't others?

"I think we have company," Kujo said. "Mount up."

"I'm not leaving without my drone," Greenbriar said.

"Leave it," Kujo said. "Swede already has the images."

"I'm not leaving without my drone," she repeated.

Bastian turned to Jenna. "Get to your ATV."

She hesitated. "I'm not leaving without you."

"I'm coming, but I'll provide cover while Greenbriar brings in her drone."

A shot rang out. The drone shuddered in the air, and then dropped like a rock, crashing into the trees.

"Time to go." Greenbriar shoved her remote control into her jacket, slammed her helmet over her head and ran for her ATV.

"Go!" Bastian yelled. "I'll cover."

While the others ran for their vehicles, Bastian took longer, backing his way to his four-wheeler, keeping a vigilant eye on the forest in the direction from which the engine noise emanated.

"Bastian!" Angus cried out. "I've got you covered now. Mount up."

Bastian turned and raced toward his ATV. The others had already left the clearing, Jenna trailing the rest and Angus on his four-wheeler, holding his rifle at the ready.

Bastian flung his leg over the seat, crammed his helmet on his head and quickly buckled the strap beneath, while pressing the starter switch.

"They're here!" Angus yelled and fired a warning round over the heads of the bikers and four-wheeler riders racing toward them from a couple hundred yards away.

Pressing hard on the throttle, Bastian left the clearing, following Angus into the woods and back along the logging trail behind the others.

Shots rang out from behind them. Bastian leaned low over his four-wheeler, praying their pursuers were too far away to hit anything.

Ahead, he could see Jenna, flying over the rugged terrain, much faster than was safe, but not fast enough to stay ahead of the men pursuing them for long.

Six streaked through the woods, far ahead but falling behind Kujo. He took shortcuts the ATVs couldn't, leaping over fallen tree trunks and ditches with ease.

Bastian held on tight, desperate to catch up to Jenna. He debated stopping where he was and setting up a defensive line with Angus to hold off the attackers until the rest of their party could get to safety.

He shot a glance toward Angus. His brother flew through the woods like a bat out of hell, hanging on to the handlebars as the four-wheeler bumped over the rugged terrain. All of his focus seemed to be on remaining upright on the ATV. How would he get his attention if they needed to stop and set up defense?

Bastian returned his attention to the woman on the ATV in front of him just in time to watch in horror as Jenna's ATV hit something solid. Her four-wheeler came to an abrupt and jarring stop. Jenna flew over the handlebars, did a complete flip and landed on her back in the brush.

His heart slammed against his ribs, and the rest of the world around Bastian grew fuzzy and out of focus. He couldn't think about the attackers behind him. All he cared about was the woman ahead, lying motionless on the ground.

CHAPTER 11

JENNA LAY STUNNED. Her helmet had been knocked off and the breath knocked out of her. For what felt like a long time, she couldn't move. She stared up at the light peeking through the canopy of leaves. Her vision swirled. Blinking seemed to help bring her back into focus, so she blinked some more.

"Jenna!" a familiar voice called out to her.

She couldn't turn to see who was calling out to her, but she knew it was Bastian.

Her heart swelled. When she opened her mouth to respond, nothing came out. A gray fog crept in at the edges of her vision.

Air. She needed to breathe.

Then, as if her body suddenly remembered how, her lungs kicked in and pulled in a massive gulp of life-giving oxygen.

Jenna gasped.

An ATV came to a skidding stop beside her, and Bastian threw himself off onto the ground where he knelt beside her. "Jenna, sweetheart. Talk to me."

"Bastian," she whispered.

His hands swept over her legs and arms. "I don't feel anything broken, but that doesn't mean anything. What hurts? Can you move?"

"I don't know," she said. "I haven't tried." Jenna moved her fingers then her toes. Then she tested the rest of her body, limb by limb.

About that time, she remembered they were being chased. Jenna jerked to a sitting position, her eyes wide. "What happened?"

She turned her head right and left.

Angus, Colin, Kujo and Special Agent Greenbriar had set up a semi-circle perimeter around her and Bastian, each positioned low to the ground, using the trunk of a tree for cover. The German Shepherd lay on the ground beside Kujo. They'd abandoned their four-wheelers and lay in the leaves, rifles in hand, aiming at the men in the distance, approaching them on bikes and ATVs.

"Get down," Bastian said.

Jenna dropped back on the bed of leaves.

Bastian threw his body over hers.

"No. You can't use your body as a shield," she wheezed, crushed by his weight, unable to shove him off.

"Shh," he said. "If you promise to stay down, I'll move."

"I promise," she said.

Bastian rolled off her, low-crawled to his four-wheeler, reached up and pulled his rifle from the scabbard. Then he low-crawled back to where Jenna lay. "I need you to stay low and behind the four-wheeler."

She shook her head, the fog clearing with the threat of danger. "I have a gun. I can help."

"You'll help more if you do as I say. You might have damaged your spine, moving could aggravate the injury."

"I'm okay." She wiggled her body, stretching her back. "See? And I have a gun. I can help." She took her handgun from the holster and rolled onto her belly. She was sore, but unharmed.

He snorted. "There's no talking sense into you, is there?"

Jenna frowned. "Not when we're outnumbered, and we can use every gun available." She nodded toward the others. "Let's join the team."

Bastian's lips thinned.

"You might as well give in," she said. "We don't have time. And if you leave me here, I'll follow anyway." She got up on her hands and knees, pushed to a low, hunkered-over position and ran toward the others.

Bastian caught up and ran with her.

When she came online with the others, Jenna dropped to the prone position next to a tree and aimed her handgun at the oncoming bikes.

The bikers out front burst through the trees, heading straight for their defensive line.

Jenna held her fire, knowing her handgun couldn't accurately hit anything as far away as they were. She counted eight aggressors.

The others let loose a volley of bullets, bringing down the lead riders. The other six slowed.

"We have their attention. Fire at their tires," Angus called out.

One of the men held up his hand and inched forward on his four-wheeler until he came abreast of one of his downed comrades. He leaned over, grabbed the man's outstretched arm and hauled him up and onto the back of his four-wheeler. Then he turned and drove off into the woods.

The five riders remaining upright revved their engines as if trying to decide whether to charge them.

Finally, one of them eased forward to the man lying motionless on the ground. He nudged the body with his toe. It didn't move.

The man on the four-wheeler turned and raced away, the other four riders following him.

Jenna breathed a sigh and slumped against the ground. Thank God they'd brought as many people as they had with rifles that had such good range.

"Bastian cover us," Angus called out.

"Roger." Bastian trained his weapon in the direction the bikers had gone.

Angus and Colin climbed on their four-wheelers and rode out to where the body lay on the ground.

Angus dropped down beside the man, checked for a pulse and shook his head.

"Is he dead?" Jenna asked, straining to see what was happening.

"I think so," Bastian answered, his gaze going past his brothers.

Jenna shifted her glance, studying the distance, watching closely in case the aggressors decided to swing back and attack from a different direction. Bastian's brothers were out in the open, exposed.

They draped the man's body over the seat of Angus's four-wheeler. Angus climbed on board, standing behind the body, and drove the four-wheeler back toward the trail.

Kujo and Six remained in their prone position. "Molly, Bastian, Jenna follow them. We've got your back."

Jenna looked again in the direction the riders had gone before she rose and ran back to where her four-wheeler rested, the front end smashed into a brush-covered fallen log.

Bastian drove up beside her. "Hop on."

She slid her leg over the back of the seat and wrapped her arms around his waist. Her body ached, and she was bruised, but she'd felt worse. And holding onto Bastian made it all worth it.

He'd been distant and unapproachable that morning, and she didn't know why.

At that moment, though, Jenna couldn't think about anything but hanging on and getting back to civilization in one piece.

The ride back to the trucks seemed to take forever.

Kujo and Six brought up the rear, remaining vigilant as they watched for a return of the gang who'd attacked their drone and then their group.

Why had they stopped coming after them? The day before, they'd chased them all the way out to the county road. And then they'd hung around long enough to chase them away from the downed bike. Today, they'd given up after one of their own was killed.

Ahead, Angus, Special Agent Greenbriar and Colin emerged onto the county road and raced toward the quarry where they'd parked the trucks and trailers.

Bastian burst from the underbrush out onto the road and followed Greenbriar and Colin.

Jenna glanced back at Kujo as he broke free of the forest and skidded sideways on gravel before straightening and gunning his throttle.

Six leaped over a log and raced to catch up with Kujo.

The two remained a little behind to provide protection.

When they arrived at the quarry, they didn't slow, but drove the four-wheelers up on the trailers before they stopped.

Jenna slid off the seat. Her legs wobbled for a moment then held. She could still feel the vibration of the engine running through her body. She suspected she'd have residual tremors for a long time afterward.

Bastian and Colin stood guard at the entrance to the quarry while Kujo parked his four-wheeler on the trailer and raised the ramp.

Angus and Kujo loaded the body into Angus's truck bed.

Everyone piled into the two vehicles, and they drove out of the quarry onto the road and back toward town.

Jenna didn't breathe easy until they entered Eagle Rock and pulled to a stop on the street in front of the sheriff's department. She wasn't used to people shooting at her or having to transport dead men in the backs of pickups.

Her head ached, and her body felt bruised all over. She was beginning to think that was the least of her worries.

. . .

Bastian felt like Linda Blair in the Exorcist. He'd turned his head in every direction so many times, he thought it would twist right off. He'd never been so glad to see the town of Eagle Rock, Montana come into view.

Sheriff Barron had just gotten out of his service vehicle when the trucks came to a halt.

Colin waved to him and called out, "Sheriff, we need your assistance."

The older man walked over, his brow furrowing. "What's the problem?"

Colin dropped down from the passenger seat and climbed into the bed of the pickup. Angus, Bastian, Kujo and Greenbriar gathered around the truck bed and the body inside.

Jenna joined them, limping slightly.

Bastian slipped an arm around her, pulling her close so that she could lean on him and take the weight off the leg she was favoring.

The sheriff drew in a breath and let it out slowly. "Wanna clue me in on what's going on?"

"We will," Angus said. "But first, can you identify this man?"

Colin pulled the black ski mask off the man's head.

"Damn." The sheriff shook his head.

"You know him?" Angus pressed.

"Yes, I do. And his daddy isn't going to be too

happy that his boy is dead." The sheriff looked around at them. "That's Brandon Fletcher."

"As in Troy Fletcher's son?" Jenna asked.

A lead weight settled into the pit of Bastian's belly. He knew about Troy Fletcher. The man was loaded and had bought his way out of every scrape he or a member of his family had ever found themselves in.

The sheriff nodded.

"Brandon's been in and out of trouble all his young life. Two years ago, his father threw a team of lawyers at his defense to get him out of serving time for manslaughter." The sheriff raised his eyebrows. "How'd he end up like this?"

"We shot him," Angus said. "He and a gang of guys dressed all in black combat gear chased us down in the woods. When they started shooting at us, we had to hunker down and return fire."

"I had a feeling he was hanging out with the wrong crowd," the sheriff said. "Well, his daddy won't have to bail him out again. I'll need you all to fill out statements and stick around town until a thorough investigation is done. Any death due to gunshot wound is an automatic investigation and autopsy."

"We'll be at the ranch," Angus said. "And if you have names of some of the folks he hangs around with, that might help in our search for our father."

The sheriff glanced at Angus, his eyes narrowing. "You think it's his gang holding your father hostage?"

Angus nodded. "They're the ones who chased Jenna away from the cabin with the torture setup, and they did it again when we returned to the cabin. They don't want us up in their business."

"That doesn't mean they have your father," Sheriff Barron said.

"We're still waiting on the results of the blood sample we took at the cabin," Bastian said. "If the blood we had analyzed is my father's, we'll be on them like bees on molasses."

The sheriff nodded. "I'll get on the horn to the county coroner's office and have them come collect Brandon's body. I'll notify the coroner he has work heading his way. And I won't notify Brandon's father until the coroner has him. The senior Mr. Fletcher is likely to take it out on anyone close at hand. I suggest you be out at the ranch when that happens."

"We will be," Angus said.

"Good. I don't want to have to call the coroner for a second time in the same day."

"How long do we have?" Angus asked.

"An hour or two." The sheriff glanced at his watch. "The ambulance will take young Fletcher to the coroner's office in Bozeman. That will take time."

"Good," Angus said. "We need to pick up a few supplies at the feed store."

The sheriff glanced around at the people on the sidewalks. "In the meantime, I'll get a blanket to cover the evidence. Unless one of Brandon's friends notifies his father first, you have a few minutes."

"We have to wait for the ambulance to collect the body anyway." Angus nodded to Colin. "I could use some help carrying feed sacks."

Kujo joined them as he clicked a button on his cellphone, ending a call. "You can load what you need in our truck. Hank and Swede said they'd like us to meet out at the White Oak Ranch as soon as we can get out of Eagle Rock."

"Do they have the results of our morning's mission?" Special Agent Greenbriar asked.

Kujo nodded.

"We could go now," Bastian suggested.

His older brother, Angus frowned toward Kujo's truck. "Can you get all five of us in your truck cab?"

Kujo grinned. "It'll be tight, but doable."

"Good," Angus said. "The sooner we know what or who we're dealing with, the better."

"Agreed," Bastian said.

"What about the feed?" Colin asked.

"It can wait until later," Angus said. "We should be back in town in less than two hours, pick up this truck and trailer and be on our way out to the ranch before Old Man Fletcher gets wind of his son's passing."

Kujo held open the back door of the truck. Greenbriar climbed in, scooted over to the middle of the seat and fastened her seat belt.

Jenna got in beside her and frowned. "There's only room for five adults in this truck. I'll stay in town." She started to get down.

Bastian gripped her hips and lifted her to stand on the floorboard. She had to hunch over to keep from banging her head on the ceiling.

Bastian sat in the seat and pulled her onto his lap. "This will work for now." He pulled the seatbelt over both of them and buckled it securely.

Jenna had to admit, she preferred to sit this way to riding a four-wheeler. Especially after she'd crashed hers. "What about the four-wheeler I was driving?"

"Don't worry about it," Bastian said. "We'll collect it another day, if it hasn't been scavenged or torched."

"Do you think it can be fixed?" Jenna asked. "I'll pay for it."

"The heck you will," Bastian said. The woman could barely afford a crummy apartment over a noisy tavern. She sure as hell couldn't afford to fix a four-wheeler that could potentially have a bent frame. "It might be cheaper to buy a new one."

She twisted in his lap, wreaking all kinds of havoc on his libido. "I insist on paying for it," she said, her brow wrinkling in such a cute way that he felt his groin tighten.

"We'll talk about it later. Right now, we need to get you to a doctor," he said.

Jenna shook her head. "I'm fine. I don't need to go. I want to see what the drone caught on video."

Bastian frowned. "You could have a concussion."

She crossed her arms over her chest. "I'm not going."

"You're not going to win that argument," Angus said, grinning at him in the rearview mirror.

"For the record, I'm not happy about that," Bastian said.

They made it to the White Oak Ranch in under twenty minutes.

Hank and Swede were waiting on the porch and came down to shake their hands. "Everyone all right?" His gaze sought Jenna. "I hear you took a tumble."

She nodded. "I'm all right."

"Are you sure? You might want to have a doctor check you over."

"Really. I'm fine." She nodded toward the house. "I'm more interested in what the drone recorded."

Hank nodded and grinned. "Come inside. Swede's been hard at work zooming in and focusing the footage. I'll let him show you and explain."

He led the way into the house and to a door that led into the basement beneath the main floor.

Bastian was amazed at what Hank had built. The rooms were filled with state of the art electronics, computers and furnishings. A long conference table took up the center of the room and an array of computers and monitors stretched across a wall. Images were projected onto a solid white wall.

Swede sat at a computer and moved his mouse, playing the video in slow motion.

"If you watch closely, you'll see the trees change colors…right…here." He stopped the video and zoomed in on the odd color alteration. "That's camouflage netting." He zoomed in again, and they could see the tiny lines of woven netting.

"And if that's not clear enough, watch this." He played the video again. A truck pulled out from beneath the camouflage netting into the open and along a road obscured by trees. Every so often, the drone caught the sharp lines of the truck between the branches. The truck eventually emerged onto what appeared to be a maintained gravel road.

Swede zoomed in on the truck, capturing the license plate. "I ran it through the Montana license registration data base. The truck belongs to an Otis Ferguson."

Jenna stiffened, and her face paled.

"Any relation to Corley?" Bastian asked her.

She nodded. "His older brother." Jenna rubbed her hands together in a nervous gesture. "Otis taught Corley everything he knew about how to treat a woman."

Bastian slipped an arm around Jenna, his heart tight, knowing what she'd suffered.

She leaned into him. "I should have known he was involved in illegal activities. I'll bet he has Corley sucked into it as well."

"Are we missing something?" Hank asked.

Bastian glanced down at Jenna.

She nodded. "You tell them."

"Corley Ferguson is Jenna's ex-husband. She has a restraining order against him. He nearly beat her to death."

"Bastard," Special Agent Greenbriar said. "They should put animals like that down. They do that to pit bulls who attack humans. Why not humans who attack humans?"

Kujo chuckled. "Remind me not to piss you off."

Greenbriar sighed. "It burns me up when people throw their weight around and pound on smaller, defenseless individuals."

Jenna lifted her chin. "Don't worry. I'm not as easily subdued anymore. I won't let him hurt me again."

Bastian's chest swelled at Jenna's courage.

Greenbriar smiled. "Good. I still think the bastard needs to be taken down."

"Do you think that Corley is a member of that group?" Angus asked. "That might be why they were targeting Jenna."

"If Otis is in it, I'll bet my last dollar that Corley is following in his big brother's footsteps," Jenna said, her lips thinning into a tight line.

"As much as I'd like to nail that bastard," Bastian said. "We need to focus on their camp and determine whether our father is being held captive there."

"They shot down the drone," Greenbriar said. "They know we were looking and might have found their hideout by now."

"Which means, they might be on the move," Angus's brow furrowed.

Colin stepped forward. "If we don't get out there soon, they'll be gone."

Bastian nodded. "Hell, they might already have moved our father."

"Which reminds me," Hank said. "The DNA results came back."

Bastian, Angus and Colin froze, all attention on Hank.

"It was a match. With a ninety-nine-point-nine percent accuracy rating, the test showed that the blood found in that cabin belonged to the person whose hair we matched it against."

"Our father," Bastian said, his gut knotting. "Which means he was alive when they held him in that cabin a couple of days ago."

"He could still be alive," Colin said.

"Or they could have killed him during the torture," Angus spoke what Bastian had thought but hadn't wanted to voice.

"No," Colin said. "He's still alive." His jaw was tight, his fists clenched. "The man is far too stubborn to die. He's hanging on, knowing we'll find him."

"It needs to be soon. He probably needs medical attention," Angus said.

"So," Bastian looked around the room, "what's the plan?"

"We go into the camp and find our father," Colin said.

"When?" Kujo asked.

"It'll be dark soon," Angus said. "We need to get into position and move in after the sun sets."

"That gives us maybe an hour to get where we need to go." Bastian started for the exit.

"Before you run out of here, you might want to gear up." Hank led them into another room that appeared to be an armory. The latest weapons were stacked in racks and on shelves, along with communications devices, night vision goggles, grenades, explosives and detonators.

Colin whistled. "Who needs the army when you have Hank Patterson in your own backyard?"

Hank chuckled. "If any of you decide to leave the military, you know you can always come to work for the Brotherhood Protectors."

Bastian nodded. "I've heard it's a good gig."

"The guys who've come to work for us aren't complaining." He grinned at Kujo and Swede. "Are you?"

"No," Swede said.

"We like that we can use the skills we trained so hard for," Kujo said. He rested a hand on Six's head. "And I can go to work every day with my best friend."

"And learn new skills that help us with our jobs protecting others," Swede said. He lifted what appeared to be a necklace out of a drawer and handed it to Jenna. "Wear that."

"What is it?" she asked. "It's not something out of a James Bond movie, is it? Is it a miniature bomb that I can use to blow a hole in a cell wall so that I can escape?" She held the necklace out in front of her, her brow twisting.

Hank laughed. "Not any of those things, although they sound like good ideas." He winked at Swede. "Make a note to come up with an exploding necklace for our next mission."

Swede shook his head. "It's a GPS tracking device. In case you get separated from the rest of us, we can find you." He removed a small disc from the same drawer. "Or you might slip that into your pocket or in your sock."

Jenna looped the necklace over her head. "You guys aren't planning on ditching me, are you?" She stared around at the men in the room. "Oh, wait, you're not taking me on this mission, are you?"

Bastian shook his head. This wasn't a mission she could tag along on.

She sighed. "Okay, I get it. I'm out of my depth when it comes to reconnaissance and combat missions, as evidenced by my spectacular crash today. But you won't have time to go all the way back to the ranch to drop me off, and I don't want any of Hank's people to have to do it either. I would rather they went with you. You know, the more the merrier." She grimaced. "I know. I'm babbling. I'm just a little scared for all of you."

Bastian pulled her into his arms. "We'll be okay. And with Hank's communications equipment, we'll be even better."

"That's right," Angus said. "We'll wait until we can sneak in under the cover of darkness. We'll locate Dad, spring him and get the hell out."

"I'll call Parker to come get you," Bastian said.

"You can stay here until he arrives," Hank said.

Bastian borrowed Hank's land line and placed the call. "Mom...Bastian. I need Parker to come out to Hank Patterson's place and get Jenna." A frown furrowed his brow. "Okay. He is? No, we need him for something else. You will? How long will it take you to get here?" He nodded. "I'll let her know. Thanks. Love you, too." He ended the call and tapped the phone against his palm. "Parker and Molly are out with one of the heifers that's having a hard time birthing her first calf. They can't leave the ranch right now, but Mom said she'd come." Bastian's brow dipped lower. "I don't know if I feel comfortable with just the two of you riding around together."

"I have my handgun. Knowing your mother, she'll

have one as well. We'll be fine. Don't worry about us."
Jenna took his hand and squeezed it. "You guys need
to get going."

"Mom said Duncan's in town." Using the phone
again, Bastian dialed his brother's number. "Duncan,
where are you?" He paused. "In Eagle Rock? Good.
Stay there. We're on our way in, and we'll need all the
firepower we can get. We'll bring you up to speed
when we pick you up." He ended the call, replaced
the phone in the receiver and glanced at the others.
"Ready?"

His brothers, Hank, Kujo, Swede and Greenbriar all nodded. They gathered what weapons,
ammo and communications equipment they
would need. Hank handed them bullet-proof
vests, night vision goggles and helmets. They
carried the items up the stairs and out onto the
front porch.

Already, the sun had sunk to the tops of the
ridges. Within the next twenty minutes, they'd be
encased in the early dusk of mountain living.

"We have to get a move on," Hank said. "I'd like to
be in position within the next hour."

While the others loaded their things into Kujo
and Hank's truck, Bastian turned to Jenna. "Please, go
straight to the Iron Horse Ranch and wait for us to
return. Be sure to lock the doors."

She shook her head. "I'm not the one heading into
danger. You are." Jenna reached up to cup his cheek

in her hand, her brow dipping in a concerned frown. "Be careful out there."

"I will."

She leaned up on her toes and pressed a kiss to his lips, and then wrapped her arms around his neck and whispered in his ear. "I love you."

Those three words hit Bastian square in the chest like a giant battering ram. If she hadn't been holding him so close, he would have staggered backward with the incredible force of them.

She loved him.

"Bastian, let's go," Angus called out.

Jenna stepped away with a soft smile. "It's okay. You don't have to love me in return. Just come back alive." Then she ran up the stairs and watched as he climbed into the SUV and closed the door.

As they pulled away, Bastian had the uncontrollable desire to throw himself out of the vehicle, run back to Jenna and crush her in his arms.

He loved her, and he wanted her to know.

What if something happened to him on this mission? What if he didn't come back alive? She would never know that he loved her.

His jaw firmed. He was a Navy SEAL. This wasn't even a wartime situation. He'd be back, and he'd hold her in his arms and tell her that he loved her and that he was ready to let go of his vow to Lauren.

Lauren wouldn't have wanted him to spend his life grieving for her. She would have expected him to move on, find love, marry and have all those children they'd always wanted.

Bastian looked back at Jenna standing on the deck, waving at them.

I'll be back, and I'll make it right.

CHAPTER 12

TEARS BLURRED Jenna's vision as she watched the vehicles leave the yard and followed the ranch road until they disappeared into the trees.

She couldn't believe she'd told Bastian she loved him.

And he'd stood there as if he was in shock.

Her heart constricted in her chest. What had she expected? The man was still in love with his dead girlfriend from high school. How could Jenna compete with a ghost?

She sank onto the porch and let the tears slip down her cheeks. No one would see her crying and would know that no matter how many Krav Maga lessons she took, she was still weak when it came to loving someone.

Bastian held her heart in his hand, and he was driving off into the unknown dangers of a survivalist camp. Those men had military-grade weapons and who knew what else.

Hank's armory filled with weapons and protective gear might not be enough to keep them safe.

For a long time, Jenna sat on the porch, letting the tears flow. She needed to release them. She'd been bottling her feelings for too long.

When the tears stopped, she wiped her face on her sleeve and looked out at the deepening dusk. Car headlights shone between the trees as a vehicle approached Hank's ranch house.

Jenna rose, an inkling of concern making her walk into the house, lock the door and watch through the window

An SUV pulled to a stop in front of the house, and Hannah McKinnon got out.

Jenna left the house, closing and locking the door behind her. She hurried down the steps and into Mrs. McKinnon's arms,

"Hey," she said, holding Jenna close. "What's all this?" The older woman held her for a long moment, and then set her at arms' length. "They're going to be all right. I know it."

Jenna sniffed. "I hope so."

"Then why all the tears?"

She stared at Bastian's mother, and more tears welled in her eyes. "I love him, and I told him I did."

Mrs. McKinnon's brow furrowed. "And he didn't say I love you back?"

Jenna shook her head.

Bastian's mother pulled her back into her arms and held her tight. "He does, sweetie. He does."

"How do you know?"

"It's so obvious, but he can't see it." She chuckled and leaned back, smoothing the hair out of Jenna's wet face. "He can't take his eyes off you. I've never seen him so concerned over any woman's wellbeing as he is over yours."

Jenna snorted. "That's just the way he is. He cares about other people."

Mrs. McKinnon smiled. "Not like he cares about you. He just needs to recognize it as love, let go of his unfounded guilt over losing Lauren and realize he has a beautiful, wonderful woman right in front of him, who can make him happy."

Jenna hugged the mother of the man she loved. "I don't know what's going to happen between Bastian and me, but I hope you will always be my friend."

"You know I will." Mrs. McKinnon wiped a tear from her cheek. "Come on. Let's get you home."

Jenna rounded the SUV and slid into the passenger seat.

Bastian's mother got in and started the vehicle, turned around in the driveway and headed back to Eagle Rock.

"Do you mind if we stop by my apartment while we're in town?" Jenna asked, a twinge of guilt nagging at the back of her mind. She'd promised Bastian they'd go straight to Iron Horse Ranch.

"Not at all," Mrs. McKinnon said. "I've always wondered what the apartments over the Blue Moose looked like."

Her lips twisting, Jenna stared out the window. "It isn't much to look at."

"But it's a start. After what you went through with Corley Ferguson, you've done well for yourself." Mrs. McKinnon reached out to touch Jenna's arm. "I'll never forget going with Molly to the hospital after what he did to you." Her lips formed a thin line. "No woman deserves that. The man should have been locked up and the key thrown away."

"I wish," Jenna agreed.

The drive into Eagle Rock didn't take long. Soon they were pulling into the rear parking lot at the Blue Moose Tavern.

Jenna and Mrs. McKinnon climbed the back staircase up to the second floor where there were four neat little one-bedroom apartments.

Music blared from the tavern below, and the sounds of laughter could be heard through the open back door to the kitchen.

Jenna unlocked the door to her apartment and switched on the light in the living room. "It's not much, but it's what I can afford for now."

Mrs. McKinnon stepped in. "It's not so bad."

"The furniture is worn, but it came with the apartment."

"I like the accent pillows you've added to brighten it." Bastian's mother strolled through the small living room, touching the pillows and a crocheted afghan. She smiled at photographs of Jenna and her parents. "Are your parents still in Florida?"

"Yes, ma'am." Jenna crossed to the bedroom and grabbed a couple of shirts and pants from her closet. She checked the voicemail on her answering machine and sighed. "I need to return these calls tomorrow. I've got to get back to work soon, or the clients I've earned will move on."

"I'm sure they'll understand. You can use the phone at the ranch. If you have to do some showings, maybe Bastian will go along with you to keep you safe."

Jenna stopped in the doorway of the bedroom. "I shouldn't have to be protected from anyone. What's wrong with people that they can't live and let live?"

"Tell me about it." Mrs. McKinnon gave her a gentle smile.

"I'm sorry," Jenna said. "You of all people have the most to be angry about. It's been weeks since your husband disappeared."

The older woman nodded. "I'm holding out hope that the boys find him tonight and bring him home."

"How can you be so calm?" Jenna asked.

"I don't want to get too excited. Over the past

couple of weeks, I've been hopeful, only to have my hopes dashed. I'll get excited when I see James walk through the door and gather me in his arms."

Jenna's chest tightened. She wrapped her arms around Mrs. McKinnon and held her for a long moment. Then she stepped back. "Let's go home."

They exited the little apartment, closing and locking the door behind them.

As Jenna descended the stairs to the parking lot, she looked around, always aware of her surroundings.

Darkness had settled over the little Montana town. The only light came from a yellow bulb glowing over the tavern's kitchen door. Nothing moved in the back parking lot, yet a cold finger slithered down the back of her spine.

Having felt that same shiver of apprehension before, she didn't shrug it off but lifted her chin and swept her gaze around the lot and the surrounding trees and vegetation, searching for whatever it was that made her uncomfortable. It was as if someone was watching her.

Jenna hurried to Mrs. McKinnon's vehicle and got in. As soon as the older woman was settled into her seat, Jenna hit the lock button on the door.

Mrs. McKinnon shot a glance her way. "You feel it, too?"

Jenna nodded. "I don't know what it is, but I get a creepy feeling sometimes."

"Like someone is watching you?" Mrs. McKinnon started the engine. "Sweetheart, you're not coming back to live in this apartment."

"I have to," Jenna said. "It's all I can afford until I start making some sales."

"You'll stay at the Iron Horse Ranch. I shouldn't have let you move out after your recovery. If I'd known how creepy this back parking lot was, I wouldn't have let you leave."

"That's nice of you, Mrs. McKinnon."

"Mom. Call me Mom or Mama Mac." She grinned, reached over and patted Jenna's hand. "You're family."

"Mama Mac, I can't just move in with you. What if things don't work out between me and Bastian?"

"You'll still be family."

"It would be awkward to hang around after a breakup." Jenna squeezed Mrs. McKinnon's hand. "But thanks. Molly and I took self-defense lessons for a reason. I can take care of myself."

They were heading out of town by that time. Dusk had long since given way to darkness.

"You think the guys are moving in around the encampment about now?" Jenna asked in the silence stretching between them.

"I hope so," Mrs. McKinnon said. "I hope a lot of things."

"Me, too," Jenna said softly. She prayed they all

returned unharmed and that they found Mr. McKinnon and brought him home to recover fully.

"I worry about you, Jenna," Mrs. McKinnon said.

Jenna snorted. "You have enough to worry about." She glanced at the woman, amazed at her strength and determination to keep going in the face of adversity.

The older woman slowed to take a curve and chuckled at the same time. "It's what I do—"

Bastian's mother's eyes widened, and she jerked the steering wheel to the right.

Jenna turned toward the road ahead in time to see a truck sitting sideways in the middle of the road, taking up both lanes of traffic. She opened her mouth to scream but didn't get it out before the SUV they were traveling in careened off the road, down into a ditch and up a rise, crashing into a tree trunk.

The strap across Jenna's shoulder tightened, as she was flung forward. Airbags deployed, slamming her back against her seat. Fine dust filled the air.

For a moment, Jenna couldn't breathe, couldn't move and couldn't see.

Then the airbags deflated. Without the dash lights, darkness was complete.

"Mom," Jenna called out, barely able to force the single word from her lungs. The seatbelt still held her so tightly that she couldn't get a full breath.

A moan sounded beside her.

Fear cleared her brain faster than a blast of arctic air. "Mrs. McKinnon," Jenna called out. "Talk to me."

Another low moan sounded.

Jenna fumbled for her seatbelt buckle, her hands shaking. When she finally found it, she hit the button. It didn't release. She hit it again and again and finally, it let go.

She dragged in a deep breath and turned toward Mrs. McKinnon. She touched the woman's arm and felt her way up to her face. Warm, stickiness oozed from a spot on her forehead.

"Mrs. M, please, talk to me," Jenna begged. The acrid scent of gasoline alerted her to the danger of staying in the vehicle. If something set off a fire, the entire vehicle could blow.

Where the hell was the driver of the truck that had been parked in the middle of the damned road? She had a bone to pick with him for leaving it there and causing them to crash. First, she had to get Mrs. McKinnon out of the SUV.

Jenna reached for the door handle and pushed. It opened a crack, but no more. She hit the window button. With no power, the window wouldn't slide down.

Again, Jenna tried the door, pushing hard with her shoulder. When her efforts met with defeat, she refused to give up. She pushed to her knees and crawled across the console into the back seat. From there, she tried the back door on Mrs. McKinnon's side of the SUV.

She pulled the handle and pushed so hard that when the door swung open easily, Jenna fell out onto the ground. When she hit, she rolled down into the ditch, coming to a stop in a cold puddle of water mixed with the gasoline leaking from the damaged tank.

Jenna came up on her hands and knees then lurched to her feet, climbing up the steep bank to the crashed SUV. She pulled hard on the driver's side door. She had to get Mrs. McKinnon out and away from the vehicle.

When the door wouldn't open, Jenna braced her foot beside the door and tried again, giving it all the strength she had.

The door opened and once again, Jenna fell backward and down into the ditch.

She rose to her feet and sucked in a shaky breath.

As she took a step toward the SUV, thick, muscular arms reached around her, a hand clamped over her mouth, and she was lifted off the ground.

She fought, kicking and wiggling as hard as she could.

The thick bands of steel around her had her arms trapped against her side. With her feet off the ground, she couldn't gain any leverage to flip her attacker. All she could do was kick and struggle until her captor loosened his hold and she could engage her Krav Maga skills.

She was carried up the embankment to the road where the truck remained parked across both lanes of traffic. On closer inspection, Jenna realized it was the truck they'd seen on the drone footage. The one that belonged to Otis Ferguson.

Jenna knew Otis. He was a mean son of a bitch, but he wasn't nearly as hulkingly large as his younger brother, Corley. Which meant...her ex-husband had caught up with her and was violating the restraining order that wasn't worth the paper it was written on.

She tried to talk, but the hand over her mouth wouldn't let her emit more than a grunt. Reasoning with the former football player would be difficult. Hell, it would be impossible. Between the head trauma of playing a full-on contact sport and the influence of a sadistic bastard of a brother, Corley wasn't a man who could be reasoned with.

Jenna quit struggling, conserving her energy for when he let his guard down, and she could pull her gun or make a break for it.

Corley shoved her against the body of the pickup and pinned her there with his weight. Then he reached for something on the truck's roof.

He let go of her arms and used both hands to deal with the item he'd reached for.

The telltale sound of adhesive being ripped from

an industrial roll of duct tape made Jenna's blood run cold.

If he bound her with duct tape, she would have no way to escape. She wouldn't be able to come back and free Mrs. McKinnon from the car and get her the medical attention she needed.

With the desperation of an animal caught in an iron trap, Jenna fought, writhed, kicked and screamed.

When Corley shifted his weight off her back, she twisted and ducked beneath his arms then threw herself beneath the truck's chassis.

"Damn bitch," Corley cursed.

Jenna rolled to the other side, pushed to her feet and took off, fumbling for her gun beneath her jacket.

She hadn't gone more than five steps when a freight train ran her over, knocked her to the ground and crushed the air from her lungs, trapping her hands between her body and the pavement.

"I should have killed you when I put you in the hospital the first time," Corley muttered in her ear, his breath smelling of whiskey.

"Get off me, Corley. You're violating the restraining order," Jenna said, her voice barely more than a whisper. She couldn't get enough air in her lungs to push past her vocal cords.

He grabbed her hair and pulled her head back

until her neck strained. "You're my wife. You belong with me, not that stinkin' McKinnon brat."

"I'm not your wife," she said, her scalp straining from the way he was pulling her hair. "Our divorce was final after you almost killed me."

He slammed her forehead against the asphalt. "You married me for better or worse. That means forever."

Pain shot through Jenna's head, and her vision blurred. "I could never be with a man who beats his wife. A man who hits someone smaller isn't a man at all."

"Shut up," he said and smashed her face against the pavement again.

Her head swam, and darkness took on an entirely different meaning. She fought the haze descending on her mind like curtains for the last call on stage.

Must...not...pass...out...

CHAPTER 13

"We're within one hundred yards of the coordinates," Hank's voice came through loud and clear over the communication device. "Bastian, report."

Bastian had volunteered to take point to recon the area before the others moved in. Lying in the brush thirty yards from the closest structure, he lowered his night vision goggles and scanned the survivalists' camp, his pulse kicking up a notch. This could be the moment when they found their father.

He stared for a long time, straining to see deeper into the camp. As he studied the area, his heart sank to the pit of his belly and hope faded.

"Well?" Angus's impatient voice sounded in his ear.

"I see tents, crates and boxes." Bastian paused. "No heat signatures."

"No heat signatures?" Colin asked. "None?"

"None." Bastian moved closer, careful to check for trip wires. He didn't know what the survivalists were capable of, or how far they would go to keep their secrets safe.

When he reached the side of the first tent, he pulled his K-bar knife from the sheath at his ankle, stabbed it into the canvas and dragged the blade to the ground. Parting the edges, he looked inside. Nothing but some cardboard boxes and food wrappers.

He rounded the tent and stood looking at the other structures. "It's like a ghost town. They must have bugged out between the time the drone flew over and when we got here."

Hank joined him along with Angus, Colin, Duncan, Kujo, Swede and the FBI Special Agent, Greenbriar.

"If you recall, we saw one truck leave the area," Swede reminded them.

"That could have been the first of many or the last one out," Hank said. "They left a lot behind."

"Yeah, but not our father," Colin said.

Angus clapped a hand on his brother's shoulder. "We'll find him."

"When?" Colin bit out.

"Soon," Angus said.

Duncan shook his head. "Mom's going to be devastated."

"She'll deal with it," Angus said. "She always does. And she has us to help her through."

"We don't seem to be all that much help," Colin said, sounding disgusted. "How much more will Dad be able to withstand?"

Bastian ducked into each of the tents and one tin shack, searching for answers. Yes, they'd left trash, but nothing else that would lead them to where they might be hiding now. He returned to the center of the compound. "There's nothing to be found here."

Hank nodded. "Let's get back to the ranch and look at the images again."

Swede shook his head. "I went over them several times. There were no other areas that stood out. If they're hiding in a cave, we'd have to see them going in or out to catch them on drone video."

"And we don't have a drone to do anymore surveillance," Ms. Greenbriar said.

"What now?" Duncan asked.

"Back to the drawing board," Angus said. "Let's get back to the ranch."

They didn't have to tell Bastian twice. He hadn't liked leaving Jenna at the White Oak Ranch waiting for someone to pick her up. The way things had been going lately, she seemed to be a walking target. He hoped his mother and Jenna had done as he'd said and gone straight back to the Iron Horse Ranch.

The sooner he got home, the better he'd feel. And

he had to come to grip with what Jenna had said right before he'd left her.

I love you.

As soon as he'd climbed into the SUV to leave, he'd wanted to go back to her and tell her that he loved her, too. He should have told her as soon as she'd said those three words. Why had he hesitated?

Eleven years was long enough to grieve. He hadn't died with Lauren, though he'd wished he had at the time. And like everyone had said, time helps heal all wounds. At least, it helped numb them. Lauren had died. He hadn't. Bastian needed to get on with the business of living.

He hurried back through the woods, anxious to get to Jenna and tell her just that. He was finally ready to get on with living. And he wanted to be with her. That cute little brat he'd found annoying as a kid had grown into a beautiful, kind woman with a heart as big as the state of Montana, and he loved her.

The team made it back to the SUV and truck, piled in and headed back to town. As soon as they were within range of the communications towers, Bastian's cellphone vibrated in his pocket.

He pulled it out as Colin, Duncan and Angus pulled out their cellphones.

Bastian stared down at the text message that came across from his sister, Molly.

911! Mom hurt. Jenna missing. Call now!

Bastian glanced up at the same time as his brothers.

"Did you get it, too?" Angus asked.

Bastian, Colin and Duncan all nodded.

"I'll call," Bastian was already hitting the number for his sister.

Molly answered on the first ring. "Bastian, are you with the others?"

"We're all here," he said, his pulse pounding so hard against his eardrums he could barely hear.

"I'm with Mom in the back of an ambulance, on our way to the hospital in Bozeman. We're heading out of Eagle Rock now, so I'll lose reception soon. She and Jenna were involved in a car wreck on the way to the ranch. They'd hit a tree. A neighbor found Mom, unconscious. She's since come to and is talking to me. The neighbor said Mom was alone when he found her. Her SUV had gone off the road on the way to the Iron Horse Ranch. The airbags deployed and the passenger side door was open but no Jenna." Molly paused.

For a moment, Bastian thought Molly had lost reception.

"Bastian, I'm worried about Jenna. Sounds like Mom was on her way back home after picking her up. Jenna wouldn't have left mom in the car after a wreck. I'm afraid someone took her. You have to find her."

Bastian's heart and fists clenched. "We'll find her.

Keep us informed about Mom," he said. "We'll join you at the hospital as soon as we find Jenna."

"Bastian," Molly's voice lowered. "Did you find Dad?"

Bastian drew in a deep breath and let it out. "No."

"I'm really sorry to hear that," she said. "I'll let Mom know when she's capable of handling it. In the meantime, I love you guys. Be safe." Molly ended the call.

"Well?"

"Mom crashed into a tree on her way back to the ranch. She's talking to Molly, but we don't know the extent of her injuries. Jenna's missing. She was in the car when Mom ran into the tree. Where she went, no one knows."

"We can find out." Swede dug in a bag at his feet and brought out what appeared to be a handheld radio.

Swede bent over the device. "We should be able to locate her quickly, as long as she's still wearing one of the GPS devices I gave her before we left earlier."

He switched on the tracker and waited while it booted. A moment later, he looked up. "Got her."

"Where is she?" Bastian leaned over the back of the seat, trying to get a look at the tracker.

"On a road three miles north of Eagle Rock," Swede said.

Hank pressed his foot down hard on the accelerator. "We can be there in fifteen minutes."

"Make it sooner," Bastian said. He didn't know who had taken her or what their plans were, but if they hurt one hair on her head... "Could you go a little faster?" he urged.

"Got the pedal to the metal," Hank said. "Going as fast as I can. As it is, we'll be speeding through Eagle Rock."

"I'll call the sheriff and let him know," Angus said. "He can bring backup."

Bastian sat forward, his gaze on the road ahead, willing the SUV to go faster.

As they blew through Eagle Rock, he prayed they wouldn't be too late.

THE SOUND of a door slamming brought Jenna awake and immediately made her want to pass out again as sharp pain rippled through her head. She opened her eyes and lifted her head, staring around a room with which she was unfamiliar.

When she tried to move her hands to push the hair out of her face, she couldn't. She didn't understand why until she looked down at her arms bound to a wooden chair with gray duct tape.

Alarm rippled through her, clearing her fuzzy mind. That's when she remembered. She'd been taken from the scene of an accident. An accident that had left Mrs. McKinnon unconscious.

Jenna fought to free her arms, but the tape had

been wound around enough to keep her arms completely immobile.

She focused on the shouts coming from another room, recognizing the voices of Corley and Otis Ferguson.

"You dumbass!" Otis yelled. "You had no business bringing her here."

"I couldn't take her to our house in town. They would have found her there."

"They'll be looking for her. Eventually, they'll find her here."

"They didn't find McKinnon," Corley said. "Why should they find Jenna?"

Jenna's pulse quickened. The Fergusons knew something about James McKinnon.

"If that bitch had come to that cabin a day earlier, she would have found him and me."

"But she didn't," Corley said. "And they didn't find him or you."

"Only because his keepers have him on the move," Otis said. "He doesn't stay in one place longer than a day or two."

Jenna's heart clenched. No wonder the authorities and the McKinnon family couldn't find James.

"If you're so damned smart, who are *they* and where are they taking him next?" Corley asked. "*They* always show up with ski masks on. How do you know they aren't part of the deep state? They could be with the sheriff's department or the state police."

"You think I'd tell you?" Otis snorted. "You can't keep your dick in your pants long enough to keep a fuckin' secret."

"It's not my fault they discovered the location of the camp."

"Yeah, if you hadn't chased after that bitch, her boyfriend and his brothers wouldn't have had a reason to expand their search beyond the cabin."

"He's not her boyfriend. She's my goddamn wife!" Corley yelled. "I'll be damned if I let her screw around with other men. She's mine."

"You lost that right when you nearly killed her. No court in this country is going to let you keep her."

"I ain't going back to court," Corley gritted out.

"You've already screwed that pooch by taking her. Now, what are you going to do with her?" Otis asked. "If she gets away, she'll have your ass in jail faster than you can say restraining order. And you'll be up on kidnapping and assault charges to boot. You're going to jail, little brother. Any way you look at it."

"She's not going to get away, and I'm not going to jail," Corley said. "You're the one who should be going to jail."

"Why should I go to jail?" Otis said. "I haven't done anything anybody knows about."

"You put the screws to old man McKinnon. If that ain't assault, I don't know what is. I've never seen a more stubborn man than that one."

"If he'd just tell them where the loot is, it'd be all

over. They're not going to keep him alive much longer. They're practically foaming at the mouth to get to that money."

"Maybe he doesn't know where it is," Corley said.

"He knows," Otis said. "The man who shot Reed was there. He said Reed whispered something to McKinnon before he died. It had to be the location of his stash."

"I don't know how they're going to get it out of the old man," Corley said. "If he didn't talk after what you did to him, he ain't gonna."

"If they let me at him again, I'll get it out of him. In the meantime, get her out of here. We gotta keep up the appearances of being on the right side of the law, even if we ain't."

"Where else am I gonna take her?"

"Take her to the camp. They should all be gone by now."

"That's a good idea. But not until after the McKinnon brothers find it," Corley said. "No. I gotta keep her here for a couple days. Once interest in the abandoned camp dies down, I'll move her out there."

A couple of days? Jenna's heart sank to her knees. Surely, she'd be found before then. Corley talked like he wanted to keep her alive, but his temper always got the better of him. If he got mad like he had that once, Jenna wasn't sure she'd live through the beating again.

"That'll take too long," Otis was saying. "You gotta

get her out of here sooner than that. Someone's gonna start pokin' around and find out this place isn't as abandoned as it looks."

"You got any bright ideas?" Corley demanded.

"You don't need the bitch, Corley," Otis said. "She's been nothin' but trouble since you married her."

"Yeah, but she's mine. I ain't lettin' no other man have her."

"Fine, you don't have to let another man have her if she's dead."

Fear struck Jenna square in the chest and rippled all the way through her body, leaving her shaking.

If Otis had his way, he'd kill her.

Jenna twisted her hands, trying to get her fingernails into the tape close to her wrist. If she could tear it just a little... She hooked the tape with her thumb and dug her nail into it, forming a small tear.

She did it again but couldn't reach much further back. Wiggling her wrist, she pulled up as much as she could. The tear grew a smidge bigger.

Between wiggling her wrist and pulling her hand up, she stretched the tape and had the tear halfway down the arm when she realized the voices had stopped and footsteps were headed her way.

Jenna slumped in the chair, pretending she was still unconscious. Her hair fell forward, veiling her face.

Through the slits of her eyes, she could see Corley enter the room.

"What am I gonna do with you, Jenna?" he said.

Jenna didn't respond. She tried to look as limp and unconscious as she could, though her body wanted to tense into fight mode.

"Otis wants me to slit your throat and hide the body."

Corley ran his hand over her hair. "I don't want to kill you. I love you." His hand dug into her hair, and he yanked her head back.

Jenna gasped and stared up into Corley's angry eyes.

"You were supposed to love me until death do us part." He glared down at her. "You promised in our marriage vows."

"Where in love, honor and cherish does beating me senseless fit?" Jenna rasped.

"If you hadn't been so stubborn—"

"No, Corley. There is no excuse for what you did to me. You don't love me. You just want to own me."

His face grew redder with every word she said. "You're mine, damn it. I keep what's mine."

"Like I said. You don't love me. You never have. A man doesn't hurt the things he loves." Jenna knew she was playing with fire, but all the frustration and pent up anger she'd felt toward this man who was supposed to protect her came out in full force.

"You're not a man at all. You're an animal. And your brother is no better. I hope you both rot in hell."

Corley's face turned an alarming shade of red, bordering on purple.

Jenna had gone too far. The only other time she'd seen him that mad was when he'd almost killed her over a broken bottle of his favorite whiskey.

"Take it back," Corley said, his voice low and dangerous.

"Take what back?" She snorted. "I can't take back the truth."

Corley's hand snapped out and backhanded her across her face so hard, she rocked in the chair and nearly tipped over.

Blood dripped from Jenna's lip, but she didn't care. "Does hitting a woman who is tied to a chair make you feel like more of a man? Why don't you untie me and make it more of an even match. My one-hundred and twenty pounds to your two-hundred and eighty. That sounds fair, doesn't it?"

"Don't do it," Otis said. "She's already proved she can whip your ass."

"She caught me by surprise," Corley muttered. "She won't do that again."

"Damn right she won't." Otis held up a gun. "Let her go. Let's see how good she is at dodging bullets."

"Damn it, Otis," Corley raged at his brother. "I told you she's mine."

"Yeah, and she just told you to go to hell," Otis

sneered. "You gonna keep a woman around who'd just as soon stab you in the face as take her next breath?"

Corley rubbed the knuckles of the hand he'd hit her with. "She won't stab me in the face."

"You have to sleep sometime," Otis reminded him.

Jenna lifted her hand, desperate to work the tape loose on her arm. She figured she didn't have much time. Otis was set on killing her. If he didn't, Corley would by hitting her once too often.

The tape ripped a little more. She worked her wrist and then her arm, careful not to draw to much attention to what she was doing. If she could get one arm free...

Then the tape broke beneath the wooden arm.

Hope swelled in her chest

"If you don't have the balls to do it," Otis said, "leave her to me. I'll take care of business and even dispose of the body."

Corley glared at his brother and looked back to Jenna. "You wouldn't stab me in the face while I slept, would you?"

"Of course not," Jenna said, keeping her arm on the chair, hoping they didn't notice the tape no longer held her.

Otis laughed. "Are you just stupid? She'll tell you what you want to hear to keep me from putting a bullet through her pretty head." He raised the gun, pointing it at Jenna's face.

"Don't." Corley stepped in front of Otis. "I'll take care of her."

"You better. You already got us sideways with the Snake Dragons for bringing attention to their camp. I doubt they'll let us know where they set up next time."

Corley's lip curled. "What do you care? They weren't the ones paying you to get the information out of McKinnon."

"I'm concerned that the trouble you stirred up will make them lose confidence in us. They might think we're loose cannons and will let others know what they're up to in the hills. And it's all because of her." He motioned with his gun.

Jenna held her breath, expecting Otis to shoot despite Corley getting in his way.

"You think they'll blame us for them having to move camp?"

"Yes, I think they will," Otis said.

"Maybe we should think about leaving the area altogether," Corley said. "Then I could take her with me."

"And she'd kill you in your sleep." Otis drew in a deep breath and blew it out his nose like a bull getting ready to charge. "I'm not leaving this area until that money is found. I want my cut of it."

"The people who paid you to work McKinnon over promise you a cut?"

"No, but if I get another chance at McKinnon, I'll

find that stash first and take my cut." Otis's eyes narrowed. "Now, do something about her, or I will. But you can't keep her here."

Otis turned and walked back into the other room.

Jenna let out a little of the breath she'd been holding. She was more afraid of Otis than she was of Corley. Now that she had one hand free, she might have a chance to defend herself, maybe even get away from the brothers.

The only problem was there wasn't a door in the room where she was being held. Just a picture window, and it was covered in dark sheeting like the cabin where James McKinnon had been tortured.

Her blood boiled at the cold, calculating way Otis talked about torturing James McKinnon. If she was going to stab anyone in the face, it would be Otis Ferguson for what he'd done to Bastian's father. James McKinnon was a tough man, but he was kind and fair. He didn't deserve what was happening to him.

"So, what's it going to be?" Corley said. "Should I do as my brother said and put you out of my misery? Or should you and I run away together and start all over?"

Jenna ground her teeth together at the thought of starting all over with Corley. But if it got her out of that house and away from Otis, she'd have more of a chance to escape. Swallowing the bile rising in her throat, she said, "If you promise not to hit me again, I'll run away with you."

Corley tilted his head to one side. "Now, you know I've got a temper. I can't promise nothing."

She bit down hard on the words she wanted to say and forced others out of her mouth. "If you promise to try, I'll go with you. We can start over."

"She's lying, Corley," Otis called out from the other room.

"Shut up!" Corley yelled back at his brother. His face grew red, and he clenched his fists. "You ain't lying to me, now, are you?" He started toward her, his lips curling back from his teeth. "I can put up with a lot of shit but lying ain't something I got patience for."

"I'm not lying, Corley," she said.

"Then tell me you love me." He towered over her, his fists clenching and unclenching.

At this point, Jenna would tell him anything he wanted to hear. Her goal was to get out of there alive.

"I love you, Corley," she choked out, though she wanted to vomit once the words left her lips.

Corley's face went from red to purple, and his eyes bulged. "You lying bitch." He cocked his arm and swung his fist.

Jenna ducked in time to avoid the brunt of the blow, but he still caught the side of her head and sent her sprawling, chair and all across the floor. The wooden chair broke into pieces. She struggled to scoot away from him, but he caught her by the hair and yanked her to her feet.

She yelped in pain. This was it. She was going to die in that house and never know if Bastian loved her.

The hell, she was. If she could get Corley's hand out of her hair, she'd throw herself out the window and make a run for the woods. It was a crappy plan, but the only one she could come up with, considering Otis had a gun, and he wouldn't hesitate to put a bullet through her head.

CHAPTER 14

"WE'RE within a half mile of our target. Stop the vehicle. We'll go in on foot from here," Hank said as he pulled off the highway onto an old dirt road with low-hanging branches.

Before the SUV came to a complete halt, Bastian was out of the vehicle and hurrying toward the location the little green blip on the tracking device had indicated.

"Bastian," Angus caught up with him and grabbed his arm. "You can't just charge in there. They might freak and kill her. We don't even know who has her, and why they took her and left our mother."

"I don't care. They're going to die if they've hurt her." Bastian shook Angus's hand free of his arm.

"Angus is right," Colin said. "We have to assess the situation and come up with a plan to save her."

"Fine. Then let's get there, assess and deal with

the bastards who took Jenna." Bastian moved out with the team.

Swede held the tracker out in front of them. "Not far now. We should be able to see—"

"House ahead," Bastian spoke into his radio headset and picked up the pace, passing Swede.

"Spread out and hold your position," Hank instructed.

Bastian came within twenty yards of the house and dropped down beside a tree.

No lights shone through the windows. A dull glow indicated the windows were covered by something dark, and lights were on inside.

Voices came from inside. Deep, male voices.

Bastian's gut twisted. Jenna was in there. His mind came up with a multitude of scenarios of what was going on in there, and none of them were good. "The windows are covered," Bastian spoke into his mic.

"I hear voices," Angus said. "It sounds like two men arguing."

"Wait," Colin's voice came over Bastian's headset. "I think I hear a woman's voice."

Bastian strained to hear it as well. There. It was a woman's voice. He couldn't tell what she was saying, but it had to be Jenna.

Then he heard the woman cry out as if in pain.

Bastian leaped to his feet, his rifle in his hands, loaded, chambered and ready for action. He raced toward the house, his focus on getting to Jenna before someone got to her first.

"Cover us," Angus said as he caught up to Bastian and ran with him. "Got a plan?" he asked.

"Get her out."

At that moment, something crashed through the window, bringing with it the dark sheeting that had covered the glass and exposing the interior of the house and two men standing in the opening. One of them pointed a gun at whatever had fallen through the window.

Bastian raised his rifle and fired at the man holding the gun.

The man stood for a moment without moving, his brow raised, a surprised look on his face. Then he fell through the window, landing on top of the jumble of black sheeting and broken glass.

The other man pulled a gun out of his waistband and aimed toward them.

Bastian and Angus dropped to the ground as a barrage of bullets flew over their heads.

The second man fell backward into the house and lay still.

"I'm getting up," he said into his mic. "I don't know if there are more where they came from."

"We've got your six," Hank said.

Bastian and Angus ran forward. Angus pulled himself up into the house, while Bastian sorted through the pile of debris on the ground.

He shoved the gunman over on his back. Light from inside the house shined down on his face. He pressed his fingers to the base of the man's throat. A faint pulse beat there. "This is Otis Ferguson. He's still alive."

From inside, Angus said, "All clear. This guy is dead."

"Did you find Jenna?" Bastian asked, leaning into the house, his gaze searching. Not finding. His heart beat fast, and his chest tightened.

"No sign of her," Angus said.

The others came forward.

Colin helped Duncan lift Otis out of the debris and laid him out on the ground. Duncan located his wound and applied pressure.

The dark pile of sheeting moved.

Bastian dug under it. His breath lodged in his lungs and hope swelled in his chest. "Jenna?"

"Bastian?" her voice came from behind the dark fabric.

He pulled it aside and found Jenna lying on her back, her arm strapped to what was left of a wooden chair, and her face bruised and bloody.

"Oh, sweetheart, you're a mess," he said.

"Not exactly the words I was hoping for," she said, raising a hand to his face.

"Let me finish." He pulled her out of the rubble and into his arms. "And the most beautiful woman I've ever known." He started to wrap his arms around her.

"Don't," she said and shoved his arms away.

"What? Are you mad because I didn't say I love you? Well, I do," he said. "I love you and want to spend the rest of my life telling you I love you."

She let out her breath. "Oh, thank God. I wasn't sure."

When he started to take her into his arms again, she held up her hands.

"Don't hold me."

He frowned. "What's wrong? Are you hurt?" He helped her step free of the debris.

"I think I have glass in my ass," she said and turned around.

A large piece of broken glass caught the light from inside the house.

"Oh, baby. You do. What do you want me to do? Leave it there and let the doctor extract it, or pull it out?"

"Pull it out," she said. "It hurts."

He tore off a piece of the dark sheeting and wrapped his fingers with it, then eased his hand around the protruding glass.

"Need some help there, Bastian?" Colin asked.

Bastian swore softly. "Give me your T-shirt."

"Huh?" Colin looked at him as if he'd lost his mind.

"T-shirt. Now," he said. "She's gonna bleed."

Colin stripped out of his jacket and pulled his T-shirt over his head.

Bastian handed him his K-bar knife. "Strips."

While Colin cut his shirt into strips, Bastian focused on the shard and not causing the woman he loved more pain.

"Just pull the damn thing out," Jenna said, between gritted teeth.

"Yes, ma'am." Bastian pulled out the glass and held out his hand. "Shirt!"

Colin handed him a strip of his T-shirt he'd folded into a neat square.

Bastian applied pressure to the wound to slow the bleeding. "We need to get you to the clinic in town. You'll need stitches."

Jenna let go of the breath she'd been holding in a long exhale. "At least you got the glass out. Think you can get the tape and chair parts off my arm?"

Bastian straightened, keeping his hand on her bottom, while continuing to apply pressure. "Hold this while I work on the tape."

He spent the next few minutes trying to ease the tape off without pulling off half of her skin with it.

"Yank it off like an adhesive bandage," she finally said.

He did as directed, hating that it hurt her, but seeing no other way.

She bit back a yelp, and the tape and wood were tossed onto the pile of debris.

At that moment, the sheriff pulled up to the cabin, followed by an ambulance.

"Perfect timing," Jenna said. "If Otis is still alive, they need to revive him long enough to interrogate him about your father. He was the one who performed the torture. Someone paid him to do it."

Bastian's teeth ground together. "If we didn't need answers from him, I'd let the bastard bleed out."

"Me, too," Jenna said. "The man inside is my ex, Corley Ferguson."

"He won't be hurting you anymore," Angus said as he came to stand beside her. "Hank and Kujo went to retrieve the vehicles. We can take you to the clinic in Eagle Rock now, or, if you can stand being in a vehicle that long, we can get you to the Emergency Room at the hospital in Bozeman."

She nodded. "I can wait for the ER in Bozeman. The clinic won't be open. They'd have to bring in the on-call. But tell me, did they find your mother?"

Bastian nodded. "A neighbor found her and called an ambulance. Molly went with her to the hospital in Bozeman. That's where we're going next."

"Is she going to be all right?" Tears filled Jenna's eyes. "I tried to get her out of the vehicle. That's when Corley caught me. I was too worried about your mother, I didn't see him until too late. He slammed my face against the pavement and knocked me out." She pressed a hand to her forehead. "I really must look a mess."

"You're not going to let me live that down, are you?" Bastian said, his throat constricting.

"Never," she said. "I might forgive you though, if you kiss me."

"I'm kind of afraid to. You're pretty banged up."

"You can kiss me here," she said and pointed to the side of her mouth that wasn't swollen and crusty with blood.

He brushed his lips across the tip of her nose instead. "We'll save the kisses for when you're not hurting so much."

"Promise?"

"I promise."

"Okay. Could we go now? I've got a splitting headache, and the other end isn't feeling much better."

Hank drove up at that moment, jumped out and held the back door for her to climb in.

Bastian assisted Jenna up into the truck, got in with her and helped her stretch out across his lap and the back seat lying on her belly.

"I'd say relax and sleep, but I'm afraid you might also have a concussion," he said, stroking her hair gently back from her face.

Jenna lay with her cheek resting on her arms. "We can talk on the way to Bozeman. You can tell me what happened at the camp, and I'll fill you in on everything Otis and Corley had to say. I think Otis had every intention of killing me. He wasn't too concerned about talking in front of me."

"Hopefully, we'll get everything out of him, and then he can die of a staph infection."

"That would be true justice," Jenna said. "You know he'd be out of jail in no time, since he hasn't actually killed anyone."

"I hope someone makes him his bitch."

Jenna laughed and winced. "Don't make me laugh. It hurts too much."

During the long trek into Bozeman, Bastian did his best to keep Jenna talking. Even so, she drifted off several times. He didn't like having to wake her, but he was afraid that if he didn't, she might never wake again.

At the hospital, she was met at the emergency room door with a gurney and rolled into a room.

Bastian insisted on going with and held her hand as the nurses stripped her out of her clothes, then cleaned her up and dressed her in a hospital gown. The doctor came in, examined her wounds, checked her for concussion and stapled the cut on her bottom.

They moved her into the same room where his mother was to observe them both throughout the night. If all went well, they'd be released the next day.

Bastian kissed his mother. "How are you doing?"

"Better now that I know my boys are okay."

"She's been beside herself not knowing what was

going on," Molly said. She sat in the chair in the corner of the room, her legs pulled up to her chest.

Bastian caught her glance and held it.

Molly nodded. "She knows you didn't find Dad."

"Mom, I'm sorry. Apparently, he never was in that camp. He was in the cabin, and Otis Ferguson was the man responsible for interrogating him."

"Does he know where James is?"

"They brought him to the hospital with a gunshot wound. When he's able, the sheriff will try to get some answers out of him."

His mother pinched the bridge of her nose. "This has to end soon. I don't know how much more he can take." She looked up at Bastian. "I don't know how much more I can take."

He held his mother's hand. "I know. I feel like we're getting closer. We just need that one piece of information that will tip the scales and blow this case wide open."

"Please, let it be soon." His mother closed her eyes. "Right now, I just want to sleep."

He kissed her cheek and moved to Jenna's bed. "Hey, sweetheart."

"Did he tell you he loves you?" his mother said behind him.

Jenna chuckled. "Yes, ma'am."

Bastian took her hand in his. "I told her. And I'll spend the rest of my life telling her, if she'll let me."

His mother lifted her head from her pillow. "Is that a proposal?"

Bastian looked down into Jenna's eyes. "Does it count if I don't have a ring?"

"Yes," his mother said.

Jenna smiled.

"To make it official, do I have to get down on one knee?" he asked.

"Yes," Molly said, dropping her feet to the floor. "Good grief, do we have to tell you everything? Ask her already. We don't have all night."

Bastian took Jenna's hand and dropped to one knee. "Jenna Meyers, if I promise to love you for the rest of my life, would you marry me?" He held up a hand before she could answer. "You need to know what that means to marry a SEAL. I still have a commitment to the Navy, and I'll be deployed more than I'm home, but when I'm home, I'll make up for all the time I'm away. And you'll likely be living on a Navy base, or close by, and have to commiserate with other Navy wives, who are in the same boat as you and miss their husbands whose whereabouts they aren't allowed to know. It's a hard life, but eventually, we'll retire here in Montana and live on the Iron Horse Ranch."

"If you're trying to scare me, you're not." She frowned. "Do you want me to say yes?"

"More than I want to take my next breath. I'd be honored if you'd be my wife."

He waited, holding his breath, praying he hadn't just shot himself in the foot.

"Yes," she said quietly and drew his hand to the not so broken side of her mouth and kissed his fingertips. "The fact you could ask me while I look like this says a lot about how you feel about me. Yes, I'll marry you. I love you, Bastian McKinnon. I think I always have."

"Then I have some catching up to do." He rose to his feet and slipped into the bed beside her, gathering her gently into his arms.

Molly sighed. "Now, that was a proposal. I hope someday I get one so beautiful."

"You will," her mother said. "You will.

The door opened, and Parker Bailey entered. "Anyone need a ride back to the ranch?"

Molly rose from the chair. "Mom, you don't need me here, do you?"

"No, sweetie. I'm sure Bastian will be here all night if I need anything. You go home and get some rest." Her mother held up her hand.

Molly took it and leaned down to press a kiss to her cheek. "I love you, Mom."

"I love you, too" her mother said. "And Parker?"

"Yes, ma'am," he came to stand beside her bed.

"Take good care of my girl. I couldn't stand to lose one of my children. She's stubborn, like her father, but she's got a heart of gold. Keep an eye on her."

"Yes, ma'am," Parker said. "I'll see you back at the ranch soon."

Bastian watched as Parker held the door for Molly, and the two left the room.

"Mom, are you trying your hand at matchmaking?" he asked, arching a brow.

"Son, I don't know what you're talking about." She closed her eyes and pulled the sheet up to her chin. "Now, if you don't mind, I think I'll say a little prayer and go to sleep. I'm sure the nurses will be in every couple of hours to make sure I'm still alive."

Bastian shook his head. With all her boys engaged now, his mother probably wanted to know her daughter would be taken care of as well.

Hell, his mother could have died in the car crash. If his father died and his mother died, that would leave him and his siblings to take care of the ranch and Molly.

No wonder his mother wanted to see Molly happily settled. And as far as he could tell, Parker Bailey wasn't a bad choice for his sister. The man was a bit older than her, but he wouldn't put up with her nonsense, and at the same time, he would never hurt her.

"You're thinking about Parker and Molly, aren't you?" Jenna whispered.

"How'd you know?" He nuzzled her neck, one of the only places that wasn't bruised.

"I have to admit. I worry about her, too. She needs

to find someone to love that will love her as much as she loves him."

"Do you think that could be Parker?" he asked.

"I don't know. If it is, I don't think she knows it yet."

"Well, I'm not going to worry about it now. We still have to find Dad."

"Yes, we do," Jenna said. "Why don't you go check and see if they were able to get anything out of Otis."

"Are you two going to be okay without me for a few minutes?"

"We'll be fine. I might be banged up, but I could still kick some ass if I need to."

"I believe it." He kissed her fingertips and slid out of the bed. "I'll be right back."

She smiled. "I'm not going anywhere without you."

EPILOGUE

JENNA AND MRS. MCKINNON left the hospital before noon the next day. Bastian and Angus drove them home and settled them on the porch with glasses of tea and cookies Angus's fiancée, Bree, had baked especially for their homecoming.

Jenna chose to stand, while Mrs. McKinnon sat in one of the rocking chairs.

Earl Monson joined them on the porch and played with baby Caitlyn, making her giggle at the faces he made.

Bastian had returned to their room later the night before with news that Otis had gone into surgery to stop the internal bleeding the bullet had caused. He wouldn't be fit to question until the following day. Sheriff Barron would fill them in on what he found after they got home.

Hank and Swede arrived at the same time as

Sheriff Barron. They got out of their vehicles, shook hands and climbed the steps to the porch to greet Mrs. McKinnon.

"We spoke to Otis Ferguson today," the sheriff said, shaking his head. "He claims he doesn't know who is holding James hostage. He said the men always showed up wearing black ski masks, much like the Snake Dragons, but they aren't related. He said the Snake Dragons only allowed him and Corley into their group because they hoped they could shed light on where William Reed hid the money he stole from the armored car."

"So, we are no closer to finding my husband," Mrs. McKinnon said.

Jenna reached for Bastian's hand. Her heart ached for the woman and her children. Not knowing was sometimes worse than finding out a loved one had died.

"The only bright spot in this is that Otis said, despite his treatment of Mr. McKinnon, he was alive when they took him away. As long as they think he knows where the money is hidden, there's a good chance they'll keep him alive."

"My sweet James," Mrs. McKinnon said, her eyes filling with tears.

Molly stood beside her mother, holding her hand. "We'll find him, Mom."

"We have a little information we found in our search on the internet," Hank said.

All gazes turned to him and Swede.

Swede nodded. "We hacked—" He shot a glance toward the sheriff. "We researched Otis Ferguson's bank accounts and found several large sums deposited from a bank out of the Cayman islands. We traced the bank account to a corporation out of Bozeman. That's where the trail goes cold. The corporation is several layers deep in other corporations. It'll take more digging to find out who actually owns the corporation. But we'll get there. It'll just take time."

"Which means," Hank said, "someone in our neck of the woods wants to know where that money is bad enough to pay others to do the dirty work to find it. Moving money around like that will eventually lead us to the people who are holding Mr. McKinnon hostage. We're close. Really close."

"Can you pick up the pace a little?" Bastian's mother asked.

"We're trying."

Jenna's eyes narrowed. "They have to be getting desperate, knowing it could only be a matter of time before they're found out."

"True," Bastian said, his brow dipping. "Your point?"

"Otis said something that has me worried." Jenna looked to Mrs. McKinnon and Molly. "He said that if Mr. McKinnon can't be tortured to reveal the location of the money, they'd have to do something else to make him talk."

"What else could they do?" Molly asked. "Torturing a person is as bad as it gets."

Jenna shook her head slowly. "No, it's not."

Mrs. McKinnon's face blanched. "You're right."

"What are you talking about?" Molly demanded.

Bastian's jaw hardened. "If you can't make a man talk by inflicting pain on him, you threaten the ones he loves, and he'll sing like a bird."

Jenna knew the men could take care of themselves. If James McKinnon's kidnappers really wanted him to talk, they'd target his wife, or his daughter.

Mrs. McKinnon squeezed Molly's hand. "We'll have to be extra careful not to go anywhere alone," she said. "That includes all of us." Her gaze encompassed all of her children.

Jenna held tight to Bastian's hand. "Trust me, I won't let you out of my sight."

"Good, because that was my plan all along." He pulled her into his arms and kissed her gently. "I don't suppose you want to accompany me to the barn, do you?"

She smiled up at him. "I could be persuaded. I'm sure there are some animals that could use some hay."

"We've taken care of all the animals for the day," Molly said.

"We'll just double-check and make sure none of them are hungry for hay," Bastian said.

"Right," Jenna said. "Hay. From the loft."

"We really did take care of all the animals," Parker vouched for them.

Bastian and Jenna ignored Parker and left the porch and the crowd of people standing around.

Behind them, Molly was explaining to Parker. "They're not going to feed the animals."

"They said they were," Parker argued. "Maybe I should go help."

"Oh, no you don't," Molly said. "Let them do it themselves. Trust me, they know how."

Jenna chuckled and leaned into Bastian. "Your sister has her work cut out, if Parker is the one for her."

"I really don't care about their love lives at this moment. I'm more concerned about ours." He walked a little faster.

Jenna's heart skipped several beats and pounded hard in her chest. "You know, it might be a little difficult to do much since I have staples in my ass."

"We'll just have to be creative."

"Mmm," she said, excitement pooling low in her belly. "Creative could be interesting."

"I bet you never thought a hay loft could be this much fun."

"I'm betting a real bed would be even better," she suggested.

"We'll explore that possibility tonight," he vowed.

Jenna didn't care where they were, as long as they were together.

THE END

Thank you for reading SEAL's Vow. The Iron Horse Legacy Series continues with Warrior's Resolve. Keep reading for the 1st Chapter.

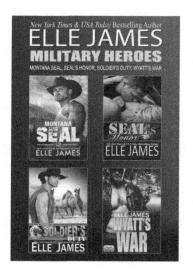

Interested in more military romance stories?
Subscribe to my newsletter and receive the
Military Heroes Box Set
<u>Subscribe Here</u>

WARRIOR'S RESOLVE

IRON HORSE LEGACY #5

New York Times & *USA Today*
Bestselling Author

ELLE JAMES

WARRIOR'S
RESOLVE

New York Times & USA Today Bestselling Author

ELLE JAMES

CHAPTER 1

"HAVE the Brotherhood Protectors dug any deeper into the corporation that paid Otis Ferguson to torture Mr. McKinnon?" Parker Bailey walked with Angus, the oldest McKinnon son, to the barn to check on the horses and throw them some hay.

"Not yet. Some corporations bury ownership so deep, it takes a court subpoena or extremely effective hacking skills to extract the information," Angus said. "Hank Patterson has Swede working on it. If anyone can hack into that corporation's database, he can. Problem is, it takes time. We're not sure how much time my father has. His kidnappers have to be getting desperate by now."

Parker frowned. "But they'll keep him alive if they think he knows where the money is, right?"

"That's what we're banking on," Angus said. "We know now that they tortured him, and he didn't reveal the location. His kidnappers will have to do something else to make him give up that data."

"Knowing how stubborn Mr. McKinnon can be, the only way they'll get him to tell is if they threaten something or someone he cares about." Parker shook his head. "He cares most about his family. You know it's only a matter of time before they target one of you. Are you ready, should that situation arise?"

Angus shook his head. "We all know to keep on the lookout for trouble. But we can't hole up and hide. We have a ranch to run, and we need to keep looking for my father."

"At the very least, you need to put your foot down with Molly. She's not following the buddy rule. You never know who'll be out there, waiting for an opportunity to snatch one of you and use you to make your father talk."

"Why don't you bring it up at dinner?" Angus said.

"I think it would be better coming from you. Your siblings look up to and respect you."

Angus grinned. "And you don't want to have to tell Molly she can't just ride out anytime she feels like it. Alone."

Parker's lips pressed into a tight line. "She doesn't listen to me. The woman would just as soon spit on me as follow any of my advice."

With a chuckle, Angus nodded. "You seem to get sideways with her a lot. Why do you suppose that is?"

"Beats the heck out of me. I try to stay clear of

her. She's a loose cannon and has a temper that gives her a short fuse."

"That's our Molly. I think my father spoiled her, being the youngest and the only girl." Angus clapped a hand on Parker's shoulder. "I would have thought as a former Air Force pararescue PJ, you wouldn't be afraid of anything."

Parker bristled. "I'm not afraid of Molly."

"No?" Angus tilted his head. "Hell, I am, most of the time. You're right. She has a temper. And when she thinks she's right, she's like a dog with a bone. She won't let it go."

"That's the truth." Parker liked that about her. She didn't back down one bit. Raised with four older brothers, she'd no doubt grown up having to defend herself against their taunts and teasing.

Angus reached the barn first and opened the door, holding it for Parker to go in first.

Once inside, Angus closed the door and looked around. "I'll get the hay. You can get the water."

"Deal," Parker said and went to the side of the barn with the hose connected to a spigot. He turned on the water and uncoiled the hose to reach across the barn to the farthest stall where Rusty, Molly's sorrel gelding, resided. Only the gelding wasn't in his stall.

Parker swore, hurried to the barn door and looked out into the nearby pasture for Rusty. When he didn't spot the horse, he ducked into the tack room and swore again.

Parker's pulse kicked up a couple notches. "When was the last time you saw Molly?" he asked Angus as he exited the tack room.

"This morning." Angus tossed hay into a stall and brushed the loose straw and dust off his hands. "Why?"

"Her horse is gone."

"She was talking about repairing that fence in the southeast pasture. Several strands were cut, and some of the cattle got through."

Parker's pulse ratcheted up, and he swore. "And I specifically told her I'd do it later today. Do you know if she at least took one of your brothers with her?"

Angus shook his head. "No. If I recall, Colin and Duncan went to town for feed and groceries. Bastian went with Jenna to look at a property."

"Which means Molly is out on the ranch by herself. And she's been out most of the day." Parker's chest tightened. "Doesn't she realize she's a prime target?"

Angus's lips twisted. "She's always been hardheaded. You can't tell her anything."

"I'll saddle up and go look for her."

"I will, too," Angus said. "There were a couple of places where the fence needed mending. We can split up and check both."

Parker led Franco, his piebald gelding, out of his stall and tied him to a metal loop on a post. Then he hurried to the tack room and grabbed a saddle, blanket and bridle.

Angus saddled Jack, the black gelding he preferred to ride during his visits home from active duty.

When they were ready, Angus opened the pasture fence and waited for Parker and Franco to pass through. He led his horse through and closed the gate, mounted and tipped his head to the north. "I'll take the northwest corner and work my way around to the south along the fence line."

"And I'll start on the southeast corner and work my way around to the north," Parker said. "Whoever finds her first should fire off a round so the other won't keep looking."

Angus nodded, nudged his horse's flanks with his heels and galloped across the pasture heading north.

Parker worried that his boss's daughter had been out all day long with no backup. The sun had already sunk low on the horizon. It wouldn't be long before it dropped below the peaks of the Crazy Mountains.

Molly should've been back at the ranch house by now. The nights were cold. Wolves and bears came out in the evening. Not only could she be a target for the people who'd kidnapped her father, she'd be hunted by the wild animals native to the Montana countryside.

His grip tightened on the reins as he urged the horse to a gallop and leaned into wind. His need to find her grew with each passing mile. Heart racing, he remembered another time he'd been sent in to rescue a Black Hawk helicopter pilot.

The mission had gone south fast. Not only did he get injured, he hadn't been able to rescue the pilot before he'd been shot and killed. The man had had a wife and two small children. Parker had never forgiven himself for being too late to save him.

His job as a member of the US Air Force's Pararescue team had been to medically treat and rescue military personnel in combat or humanitarian environments.

On that last mission, he'd failed, and his injury had caused him to be medically retired from service.

Thankfully, James McKinnon had seen something in him that Parker had thought he'd lost, and hired him on the spot.

He'd known Molly for all of the five years he'd worked at the Iron Horse Ranch. When he'd first come, she'd been a thorn in his side, always hanging around, giving him advice on how they did things there. He'd soon learned she was as smart as a whip and one of the best ranchers he'd ever known.

Her family didn't give her enough credit for all she did and all she knew about caring for the animals her family owned. So many times, because she was a woman, they didn't think she was fully capable of ranching.

While her brothers had all gone off to the military, following in their father's footsteps, Molly had stayed on Iron Horse Ranch and had learned everything there was to know about ranching, from calving, branding and worming to managing the books. She'd even brought the ranch's banking and bookkeeping into the twenty-first century by transferring the data from old manual ledgers to computer software. She'd had to drag her father along, kicking and screaming, metaphorically speaking.

As much as Parker wanted to dislike the boss's daughter, he had great respect for her abilities. She was the kind of woman he could see himself with— smart, physically strong and beautiful.

If only she wasn't the boss's daughter.

When Parker had signed on with James McKinnon as his foreman five years ago, Molly had just graduated college with an accounting degree and a minor in animal husbandry. The fresh-faced college grad came home and dove into ranching with a passion. She was beautiful, young and a threat to Parker's focus. He'd promised himself he wouldn't get involved.

To keep his promise to himself, he treated Molly like a pesky kid sister, irritating the fire out of her every chance he got.

A smile briefly tugged at the corners of his lips as

he rode across the pasture toward the southeastern border of the massive Montana ranch, tucked into the foothills of the Crazy Mountains.

He might be overreacting about the danger Molly could be in, but he'd rather be safe than have her kidnapped to force James McKinnon into telling his abductors anything.

He urged his horse to go faster.

Molly McKinnon hammered horseshoe-shaped nails into a wooden fence post, securing the strand of barbed wire she'd just stretched over one hundred feet. It was the last strand. Once she released the pressure from the come-along and packed away her tools, she'd head home.

She should have been home hours ago, but she'd spent much of her day herding the Iron Horse cattle back inside the confines of the ranch's fence. Once they were back on the right side, Molly had gone to work stretching the barbed wire that had been cut and patching it where it no longer fit.

Hot, sweaty and way past hungry, she brushed hair out of her face that had slipped from her ponytail. She straightened, working the kinks out of her back, and glanced at the clear blue Montana sky. The sun was just touching the mountain peaks. It wouldn't be much longer before the rays dipped below the ridges and sank below the other side.

Darkness came early to the mountain valleys. She'd need to head back to the ranch house soon or be caught out after dark. Not that she was afraid of the dark. Her concern was more a matter of being respectful of what lurked in the shadows. Wolves and bears moved around at night. She had her rifle in the holster on her saddle, if she needed to defend herself from four-legged animals, as well as the two-legged kind.

She'd just packed the hammer and bag of nails in her saddlebag and tied the come-along to the back of the saddle. With her foot in the stirrup, about to pull herself up onto her horse Rusty, she heard the roar of engines coming from the nearby woods.

Rusty's ears flattened, and he reared, whinnying sharply. Caught with only one foot in the stirrup, Molly fell backward, landing so hard on her back that all the air left her lungs in a whoosh.

Before she could recover, Rusty turned and raced away…with her rifle.

Two ATVs leaped out of the tree line and sped straight for her.

Molly sucked in a breath, shot to her feet and ran. She aimed for a copse of trees, hoping to duck in and hide before the ATV riders reached her.

Running as fast as she could in her cowboy boots, she could hear the four-wheelers behind her, catching up.

A glance over her shoulder made her yelp and run faster.

One of the men slowed, raised his right hand with a gun in it and fired.

Something stung the back of Molly's neck. It didn't feel like a bullet. She reached back and touched something that felt like a dart. She plucked it out of her skin, realizing it was either a poison dart or one laced with a drug to make her...sleepy.

Molly stumbled, her head getting heavy, her feet hard to lift from the ground.

The four-wheelers circled her, forcing her to stop running. It seemed like everywhere she turned an ATV blocked her path. The more she spun, the dizzier she became.

Just when she thought she might fall, a shot rang out from a distance.

One of the men on the ATVs jerked, his hand leaving the handlebar, his ATV veering out of the tight circle he'd been holding around Molly.

Molly took that moment to lunge through the gap. She staggered, ran and fell to her knees.

Another shot rang out.

The men on the ATVs turned and raced for the woods.

In the gathering dusk, a horseback rider charged toward Molly.

She pushed to her feet and ran, fear making her heart pound hard in her chest. Her breathing ragged, she fought to fill her lungs and keep moving, though every step was like walking through a thick mire of mud.

Molly wanted to lie down on the ground and sleep.

"Molly!" a familiar voice shouted. "Take my hand."

She looked up into a familiar face. "Parker? What are you doing here?" she asked, though her words slurred, and her vision blurred.

"Take my hand, dammit!" he shouted.

That's when she noticed he held out a hand.

Automatically, she placed hers in his.

"Put your foot in the stirrup. Hurry!"

"Why are you yelling at me?" she grumbled, while trying to place the toe of her boot into the empty stirrup, but she couldn't quite reach it.

His hand wrapped tightly around hers. "Focus, Molly. They're coming back. We don't have time to miss."

She narrowed her eyes and concentrated on placing her foot into the stirrup. Once it was there, she was yanked up onto the saddle in front of Parker, landing hard in his lap.

Finally, she could relax and stop running. Molly melted into his arms and lay her cheek against his shoulder.

Parker wrapped an arm around her. "Hold onto the saddle horn. It's going to be a rough ride."

With one hand on the horn and the other encircling Parker's waist, she held on as best her fuzzy mind could allow.

The horse leaped forward and broke into a gallop.

"Rusty," she said.

"Is on his way back to the barn. I passed him on my way here."

"Can't...stay...awake," Molly said, though her tongue felt like it was swollen and uncooperative.

"You have to," Parker urged. "We're being followed. And they have guns."

"I know," she said. "Shot me...dart."

Parker swore and reined the horse toward a line of trees. Hooves pounding in the ground felt like they were pounding into her head and her entire body. She wanted the world to stop and let her just sleep. *But no.*

Parker kept up the pace.

The roar of four-wheeler engines sounded behind them, moving closer.

When they reached the trees, Parker didn't slow. Several times he ducked, pushing her head down to avoid a low hanging branch.

Still, the ATVs drew nearer.

"Hold on tight," Parker urged.

He aimed the horse toward a steep embankment that dropped down sharply into a narrow valley.

The horse balked, and then stepped over the edge, slipping and sliding downward, loose gravel and dirt cascading down with them.

Molly clung to Parker as he swayed in the saddle, guiding the horse on a path barely wide enough for the horse's hooves. Certainly not wide enough for a four-wheeler.

When they reached the bottom, the horse stretched his legs and raced across a meadow and into the shelter of yet more trees.

The engine noise faded behind them but continued to follow at a distance.

Molly glanced up at the trail they'd left. Two men on ATVs drove parallel to them from above, tracking them as they moved through the valley.

Franco emerged into a wide-open pasture, and Parker gave his piebald gelding his head.

The horse flew across the field, heading for the barn.

Another horseback rider appeared from the north and ran beside them.

Parker jerked his head toward their rear and shouted to the other rider. "Trouble!"

As the other rider turned, the setting sun illuminated his face, and Molly finally recognized the man as her oldest brother.

Angus slowed his horse and drew his rifle out of the scabbard beside his knee. He aimed it in the direction of the hills and the sound of the ATVs.

Molly looked over Parker's shoulder, wanting to tell her brother to be careful.

The four-wheelers burst from a trail, heading toward her brother.

Shots rang out.

The ATVs spun and headed back into the trees.

Angus remained where he was for a few moments longer, his weapon raised and ready.

When the ATVs didn't reappear, he turned his horse and raced after Parker and Molly.

Molly sighed and leaned into Parker.

He smelled of aftershave and leather.

She liked that. No fancy cologne, just Parker, the Montana range and a setting sun. What more could a girl want?

She closed her eyes, the rocking, pounding motion of the horse making it harder and harder for her to stay awake.

Finally, they arrived at the gate to the barnyard.

Her mother rushed forward and opened the gate, her horse beside her. "What happened?" she cried out. "When Rusty came back without Molly, I was worried. I was about to come out looking for her."

"I'm not sure what's wrong with her," Parker said. "She can barely hold her head up."

"Sleepy," Molly murmured.

Angus rode through the gate behind them, leaped down from his horse and reached up to catch Molly as she slipped out of Parker's arms. He let her feet touch the ground, then slung one of her arms around his shoulder and wrapped an arm around her waist.

"Hey, bro," she slurred. "Just put me down here. I need a nap."

"Drugged," he said, his lips forming a thin line.

Parker dropped to the ground beside Angus. "I'll take her up to the house."

Molly's legs gave out. "Don't know why nothing's working. Probably because I'm sleepy."

Parker scooped her up into his arms. "I'll get her to her room, if you can take care of the horses."

Angus frowned. "The horses can wait. I want to know what they did to her."

"I'll call the doctor," Molly's mom said and raced ahead of them toward the house.

Molly closed her eyes for a second. When she opened them again, Parker was laying her on the couch and pulling off her boots.

"Need to take care of Rusty," she said, though her words came out as no more than a whisper. When she tried to sit up, her body didn't respond. She lay like a limp rag doll, unable to move even a finger.

"Your brothers will take care of your horse. Just lie still. The doctor's on his way."

"Don't need a doctor," she said. "Just need a nap." Again, she closed her eyes. "Anyone ever tell you that you smell good?"

Parker's chuckle warmed what was cold inside her and made her relax. "Why do you hate me?" she whispered.

"I don't hate you," he said quietly.

"Sure act like it," she groused.

"Shhh. You're going to be all right," he said, as if soothing a child.

"Because of you." Her eyelids were so heavy now she couldn't open them. Molly embraced the darkness and let her mind and body slip away. Later, she'd worry about those men who'd shot her and why Parker was all of a sudden being nice to her.

ABOUT THE AUTHOR

ELLE JAMES also writing as MYLA JACKSON is a *New York Times* and *USA Today* Bestselling author of books including cowboys, intrigues and paranormal adventures that keep her readers on the edges of their seats. When she's not at her computer, she's traveling, snow skiing, boating, or riding her ATV, dreaming up new stories. Learn more about Elle James at www.ellejames.com

Website | Facebook | Twitter | GoodReads | Newsletter | BookBub | Amazon

Or visit her alter ego Myla Jackson at mylajackson.com
Website | Facebook | Twitter | Newsletter

Follow Me!
www.ellejames.com
ellejames@ellejames.com

Beneath the Texas Moon

51459566R00153